"You're worried aren't you?"

"Yes," Damian admitted. "He's changed, Jessica. He's not himself anymore."

"He's the real reason you hired me, isn't he? You think I might be able to...help him." It wasn't a responsibility she welcomed or wanted.

She was about to explain all of that when she noticed the way his mouth quirked into an amused smile. Instead, she told him sharply, "I'm not a silly fourteen-year-old anymore—a girl infatuated with an older man. What I felt for your brother was just a crush. It was over years ago."

That's the simple truth, she thought. *But what I feel for you...*

"Sure." Damian's shrug was noncommittal.

"You did hire me because of Evan, didn't you?"

It took him a long time to answer. "Sometimes I wonder."

Did you two have a chance to talk about old times?"

Debbie Macomber was born in Washington State, where she still lives with her husband, Wayne, and youngest son, Dale, eighteen, and their dog, Peterkins. Her daughter Jenny, twenty-two, is married, and daughter Jody, twenty-three, is living and working in Seattle. Son Ted, twenty, is in the Army Airborne Rangers, and is engaged to be married at Christmastime. Debbie's successful writing career started in childhood, when her brother copied—and sold!—her diary. She's gone on to a considerably wider readership since then, as a prolific and popular author published in several different romance series. She says she wrote her first book because she fell in love with Harlequin Romance novels—and wanted to write her own.

Debbie loves to hear from her readers. You can write to her at: P.O. Box 1458, Port Orchard, Washington 98366.

Books by Debbie Macomber

READY FOR ROMANCE
Debbie Macomber

Harlequin Books

TORONTO • NEW YORK • LONDON
AMSTERDAM • PARIS • SYDNEY • HAMBURG
STOCKHOLM • ATHENS • TOKYO • MILAN
MADRID • WARSAW • BUDAPEST • AUCKLAND

For Jessica, who caught the wedding bouquet first

ISBN 0-373-03288-9

READY FOR ROMANCE

PROLOGUE

JESSICA KELLERMAN looked both ways, then slipped around the corner of the Dryden four-car garage. She flattened her body against the wall and moved cautiously, one infinitesimal step at a time. It was vital no one see her.

Evan's vehicle, a fancy sports car, was parked just outside the garage—and in direct view of the house. She needed to be quick.

Squatting down by the side mirror, she withdrew a bright red tube of lipstick from her pocket, opened it and heavily outlined her lips. Taking a soft white rag from the pocket of her jeans, she wiped his mirror clean and then kissed it several times. The imprint of her mouth was left in bold red.

Jessica sighed with satisfaction as she carefully opened the door on the driver's side and crawled into the front seat. The mirror over the dash was next. Her heart was pounding hard and fast, but it wasn't entirely due to her fear of being discovered. Her heart rate tended to accelerate whenever she thought about Evan.

There wasn't a man in all of Boston who could compete with Evan Dryden. To think she'd lived next door to him all these years and hadn't noticed until recently what a gorgeous hunk he was! As far as Jessica was concerned, he was the handsomest man in the universe.

She remembered the exact moment she had realized her destiny. She hadn't been the same since. The Dryden estate, Whispering Willows, was next to her own family's, and she'd often spent time in the huge oak tree spying on the two brothers. Damian was in law school now and Evan in college. Being an only child, Jessica was left to invent her own amusement, and spying on the Dryden brothers had always been great fun.

Jessica had been sitting in the tree one day when Evan had walked to the pond and stood on the footbridge tossing rocks into the water. His back was to her and she held her breath, wondering if he'd seen her hiding in the thick foliage.

She must have made a sound, because he turned abruptly and stared into the tree.

"Jessica?"

She didn't dare move or even breathe.

He stared upward and the sun cut across his shoulder, highlighting his handsome features. It was then that she realized Evan wasn't just an ordinary boy. He was an Adonis. Perfect in every way.

After that she started having dreams about him. Wonderful dreams about him falling in love with her. Dreams about them marrying and having a family. It seemed so...so right. It came to her about a week later that fate had thrown them together. They were meant for each other. The only problem was that Evan had yet to make this discovery for himself.

Jessica had recently turned fourteen and Evan was much older. Six whole years, but it might have been a hundred for all the notice he gave her.

That was when Jessica decided she had to take matters into her own hands. She was a woman of the world, and when a woman knew what she wanted, she went after it. It, in this case, was Evan Dryden.

Jessica soon discovered she wasn't nearly as dauntless as she would have liked. She must have phoned him ten times or more, and each time he answered, she lacked the courage to so much as speak, much less tell him about her undying love. Each call had ended with her replacing the receiver and stewing in frustration.

She'd always been better at expressing herself with the written word, so she'd taken to writing him love notes, pouring out her devotion. She let her best friend read one such note, and the girl claimed it was the most beautiful love letter she'd ever seen. Unfortunately, Jessica hadn't found the courage to sign her name.

This latest trick, planting kisses on his rearview mirror, was sure to accomplish what nothing else had. He'd know it was Jessica and he'd finally come for her, and together they'd ride into the sunset in his sports car.

Outlining her lips with a fresh coat of brilliant red, Jessica was about to kiss the interior mirror when the car door was flung open.

"So it *is* you."

Her heart sank all the way to her knees. Slowly she looked over and her eyes connected with Damian Dryden's. He was taller than his younger brother, dark and handsome in his own way. She was certain the day would come when some girl would feel as strongly about him as she did about Evan.

"Hello," she said, pretending it wasn't the least bit out of the ordinary for her to be sitting in his brother's car kissing the mirrors.

"You're the one, I bet, who's been phoning at all hours of the night."

"I've never called past ten," she denied heatedly, then realized her mistake. It probably would have been best to pretend she didn't know what he was talking about.

"The notes on Evan's windshield have been from you, too, haven't they?"

She could have denied that, but it wouldn't have done any good. Feeling trapped in Evan's car, she swung her legs around and gingerly climbed out. "Are you going to tell him it was me?"

"I don't know," Damian said thoughtfully. "How old are you now?"

"Fourteen," she said proudly. "I know Evan's older, but I was hoping he'd be willing to wait for me to grow up so we could get married."

"Married!"

Damian made the word sound ludicrous and Jessica bristled. "Just wait until you fall in love," she challenged. "Then you'll know."

"You aren't in love with Evan," he said gently. "You're too young to know about things like that. You're infatuated with him because he's older and—"

"I most certainly do love Evan," she flared, stuffing the lipstick tube in her pocket. She wasn't about to stand there and let him ridicule her. She might only be fourteen, but she had the heart of a mature woman and she'd made her decision. Someday she would marry Evan Dryden, and nothing Damian could say or do would stand in her way.

"I'm sure my brother's flattered by your devotion."

"He should be. The man who marries me will see himself as the luckiest man in the world." Her words were fed by pure bravado.

Damian laughed.

Jessica had been willing to overlook his earlier statements, but this was unforgivable. Hands braced against her hips, she glared at him with all the indignation she could muster, which at the moment was considerable.

"You might be older than Evan, but you don't know a thing about love, do you?"

Her question appeared to amuse him, and that only served to irritate her further.

"When a woman makes up her mind about a man, nothing can change the way she feels. I've decided to marry your brother, and not a thing you say or do will have the least effect, so save your breath. Evan is my destiny."

"You're sure about this?"

At least he had the courtesy to wipe the grin off his face.

"Of course," she said confidently. "Mark my words, Damian Dryden. Time will prove me right."

"Does my brother have a say in this?"

"Naturally."

"What if he decides to marry someone else?"

"I . . . I don't know." Damian had zeroed in on her worst fear—that Evan would get married before she had a chance to prove herself.

"There's something else you haven't considered," Damian said.

"What's that?"

He grinned. "I just might want to marry you myself."

CHAPTER ONE

JESSICA KELLERMAN'S time of reckoning had arrived. For the first time in eight years she was about to face the Dryden brothers. Evan didn't concern her. She suspected he wouldn't even remember what a nuisance she'd made of herself. Then again, he just might. But Damian was the brother who worried her most. He was the one who'd caught her red-handed. He was the one who'd mocked her and suggested her devotion to his brother was a passing fancy. Now she was forced to face him and admit he'd been right. She sincerely hoped Damian would have the good grace not to drag up the past.

Swallowing her dread, Jessica walked into the high-rise office building in the most prestigious part of downtown Boston. The building was new, with a glistening black-mirrored exterior that towered thirty stories above the ground. The Dryden law firm was one of the most distinguished in town, and in Boston that was saying something.

Jessica's footsteps made tapping sounds against the marble floor in the lobby. Although she'd been in this part of town often—the university wasn't far from the business section—this was the first time she'd been inside the impressive building.

She was nervous, and rightly so. The last time she'd spent any time with either of the Dryden brothers she'd been caught kissing rearview mirrors.

Looking back, she knew she'd been a constant source of amusement to the brothers and their respective sets of parents, as well. Young love, however, refused to be denied. Risking her family's censure, Jessica had diligently sought Evan's heart all through high school. It wasn't until Benny Wilcox asked her to the graduation dance that she'd realized there were other fish in the sea. Sweet, attentive, good-looking ones, too. Yes, Evan had been the man of her dreams, the one who'd awakened her to womanhood. She held her love for him in a special place in her heart, but was more than willing to forget the way she'd embarrassed herself over him, praying he did, too.

Although Jessica had let her infatuation with Evan die gracefully, neither set of parents had. Particularly, Lois and Walter Dryden. They thought the way Jessica felt about Evan was "cute," and they mentioned it every now and again, renewing her embarrassment.

When Walter Dryden heard that Jessica had recently graduated from business college with a certificate as a legal assistant, he'd insisted she apply with the family firm. In the beginning Jessica had balked, but jobs were few and far between just then, and after a fruitless search on her own, she'd decided to swallow her pride and face the two brothers.

She was warmly greeted by the receptionist, who gave her a wide smile. Jessica smiled back, hoping she looked composed and mature. "I have an appointment with Damian Dryden," she said.

The woman, who appeared to be in her early thirties, with large blue eyes and a smooth complexion, glanced at the appointment book. "Ms. Kellerman?"

"That's right."

"Please have a seat and I'll let Mr. Dryden know you're here."

"Thank you." Jessica sat in one of the richly upholstered chairs and reached for a *People* magazine. She'd dressed carefully for this interview, choosing a soft dove gray suit with a double-breasted jacket. The silver-dollar-size buttons were made from mother-of-pearl with flashes of deep blue and white. She wore high heels, hoping to seem not only professional, but sophisticated. Her glossy brown hair was sophisticated, too, cut in a flattering pageboy. She'd grown up, and it was important Damian know that.

Jessica hadn't even scanned the magazine's contents page when the elder Dryden brother appeared. She'd seen Damian often, from a distance, but this was the first time they'd spoken in months, possibly years. She'd forgotten how tall he was, with broad shoulders that tapered to slim hips. She remembered how much he enjoyed football as a teenager, and how good he was at tackling the opponent. From what she remembered about Damian, he preferred to tackle problems head-on, too. She knew him to be aggressive, hardworking and ambitious. He'd taken over the leadership of the law firm upon Walter Dryden's retirement three years earlier, and the firm, which specialized in corporate law, had thrived under his leadership.

"Hello, Jessica. It's good to see you again," Damian said, stepping forward.

"It's good to see you, too." She stood and offered him her hand.

He clasped it with both of his own. He wasn't an especially large man, and at five eight she wasn't especially small, but her hand was dwarfed in his. His grip was solid and strong, like the man himself.

"I've come to talk to you about a position as a legal assistant," she said. The direct approach would work best with Damian, she felt.

"Great. Let's go to my office, shall we?"

She was struck by the rugged timbre of his voice. It exuded confidence, sounding deep and firm. Little wonder Damian was one of the most sought-after corporate attorneys in Boston.

He motioned her to be seated, then walked around behind the deep mahogany desk and claimed the black leather chair. He tilted it back slightly, conveying ease and relaxation.

Jessica wasn't fooled. She sincerely doubted that Damian knew how to relax. His mother, Lois, had often voiced her concern about her elder son, complaining that Damian worked too many hours.

"Thank you for seeing me on such short notice," Jessica said, crossing her legs.

"It's my pleasure." He rolled a pen between his palms. "I understand you recently graduated from college."

She nodded. "I have a degree in early-American history."

The motion of the pen between his palms froze and a frown creased his brow. "Unfortunately we don't have much call for historians here at the firm."

"I realize that," she said quickly. "About halfway through my senior year, I realized that although I love history, I wasn't exactly sure what I planned to do with my degree. I toyed with the idea of teaching, then changed my mind."

"And you want to be a legal assistant now?"

"Yes. I was dating a law student and I discovered how much I enjoyed law. You see, we often did our homework together. But rather than register for law school and invest all that time and effort, I decided to work as a legal assistant—sort of get my feet wet and then decide if becoming an attorney is what I want to do. So I went to business college and got a certificate." She said all this in an eager rush. "Your father suggested I come and talk to you," she added, winding down. She opened her purse and produced her certificate for his inspection.

"I see." The pen was in motion again.

"I'm a hard worker."

Damian smiled fleetingly. "I don't doubt that."

"I'll work any hours you wish, even weekends. You can put me on probation if you want." She hadn't meant to reveal how much she wanted the position, but despite her resolve, she couldn't keep the anxiety out of her voice.

"This job means a great deal to you, doesn't it?"

Jessica nodded.

"I think," Damian said casually, "you're still infatuated with my brother."

He spoke as if it had been only a few days since she'd all but thrown herself at Evan. Heat radiated from her cheeks. "I... I don't believe that's a fair statement."

Damian smiled shrewdly. "You've had a crush on Evan for years."

"Perhaps, but that has nothing to do with my applying for a position here." She closed her mouth and collected her composure as best she could. She should have known Damian wouldn't conveniently forget their encounter all those years ago.

"It's true, though, isn't it?" Damian seemed to take delight in teasing her, which infuriated Jessica. She clamped her mouth shut, rather than argue with the man she hoped would employ her. "I was there the day you put kisses all over his rearview mirror, remember?"

Not trusting herself to speak, she nodded.

"I watched you look at him with those big worshipful eyes. I've seen plenty of other women do the same thing since, all gazing at my younger brother as though he were an Adonis."

Jessica's eyes widened at the use of the term. That was exactly the way she'd viewed Evan. A Greek god.

"It's true isn't it, or are you going to deny it?"

Jessica's mouth refused to work. She opened and closed it a number of embarrassing times, not knowing how to respond, or if she should even try.

Cathy Hudson, her best friend, had claimed it wasn't a good idea to apply for work with a family who knew her so well. Jessica was about to concede that Cath was right.

"I did have a schoolgirl crush on your brother at one time," she confessed, "but that was years ago. I haven't seen Evan in...heavens, I don't remember. Certainly not any more often than I've seen you. If you believe my past feelings for Evan would hinder my performance as a legal assistant, then there isn't anything more I can say—other than to thank you for your time."

Damian's smile was slightly off kilter, his eyes bemused as if, despite himself, he'd admired her little speech. Slowly a look of sadness crossed his face. "Evan's changed, you know. He isn't the man you once knew."

"I'd heard from my mother that he's been unhappy recently." She didn't know the details and hoped Damian would fill in the blanks.

"Do you know why?"

"No."

Damian gave a soft regretful sigh. "I might as well tell you, since you'll find out soon enough yourself. He was in love possibly for the first time in his life, and it didn't work out. I don't know what caused the rift, and neither does anyone else, not that it matters. Unfortunately, though, Evan can't seem to snap out of his depression."

"He must have loved her very much," she whispered, watching Damian. He was genuinely concerned about Evan.

"I'm sure he did." Damian frowned, apparently at a loss as to how to help his brother, then shook his head. "We've ventured far from the subject of your employment, haven't we?"

She straightened and folded her hands in her lap, wondering if Damian would take a chance and hire her. She was a risk, too, fresh out of school, with no job experience.

"You're sure you want to work here?" he asked, studying her with a discerning eye.

"Very much."

Damian didn't immediately respond. His silence made her uncomfortable enough to want to fill it with something, even useless chatter. "I know what you're thinking," she said breathlessly. "In your eyes I'm a love-struck fourteen-year-old, convinced your brother and I are meant for each other." She shook her head. "I don't know what to say to convince you I've grown up, and that nonsense is all behind me, but I have."

"I can see that for myself." A glint of appreciation sparked in his eyes. "As it happens, Jessica, you're in luck, because the firm could use another legal assistant. If you want the job, it's yours."

Jessica resisted vaulting out of the chair and throwing her arms around Damian's neck to thank him. Instead she promised, "I won't let you down."

"You'll be working directly with Evan," he replied, still studying her closely.

"With Evan?"

"Is that a problem?"

"No... No, of course not."

"Just remember one thing. It doesn't matter how many years our parents have been friends. If you don't do your job and do it well, we don't have room for you here."

"I wouldn't expect you to keep me on if I didn't pull my weight," she said, trying hard not to sound defensive.

"Good." He reached for the intercom and glanced at her. "When would you like to start?"

"Now, if you want."

"Perfect. I'll ring Mrs. Sterling. She's Evan's secretary, and she'll show you the ropes."

Jessica stood and extended her hand. "You won't be sorry, I promise you." She pumped his hand enthusiastically until she realized she was overdoing it.

Grinning, Damian walked around to the front of his desk. "If there's anything I can help you with, let me know."

"I will. Thank you, Damian."

She hadn't meant to call him by his first name. Theirs was a professional relationship now, but it *was* difficult to think of him as her boss. A personal bond existed between them, but until this interview Jessica hadn't realized it was there. To her surprise she found she had no such problem regarding Evan.

She and Damian walked out of the office together and down the corridor to a door with Evan's name engraved on a gold plaque.

Damian opened the door for her and allowed her to precede him. Jessica's gaze fell on Evan's secretary. The woman was middle-aged, with sharp, but not unattractive, features. She seemed to breathe efficiency. One look and Jessica was confident this woman could manage Evan's office and the entire law firm if necessary.

"Mrs. Sterling," Damian said, "this is Jessica Kellerman, Evan's new legal assistant. Would you show her around and make her feel at home?"

"Of course."

Damian turned to Jessica. "As I said earlier, come to me if you have any problems."

"Thank you."

"No, Jessica," he said cryptically on his way out, "thank *you*." The door made a small clicking sound as it shut.

Mrs. Sterling rose from her chair. She was a small woman, barely five feet, a stark contrast to tall and slender Jessica. Her salt-and-pepper hair was cropped short, and she wore a no-nonsense straight skirt and light sweater.

"I'll show you where the law library is," Mrs. Sterling said. Jessica glanced toward the closed door, wondering if Evan was in. Apparently not, otherwise Damian would have made a point of letting his brother know Jessica would be working for him.

The secretary led the way out of the office and down the hall. The library was huge, with row upon row of thick dusty volumes. Long narrow tables with a number of chairs were scattered about the room. Jessica knew she'd be spending the majority of her research time here and was pleased by how pleasant it was. She noticed the faint scent of lemon oil and smiled as she saw various types of potted plants set here and there, including a speckled broad-leaved ivy that stretched across the top of one large bookcase.

"This is very nice."

"Mr. Dryden has worked hard to make sure our work environment is pleasing to the eye," the woman remarked primly.

"Damian's like that," Jessica murmured.

"I was speaking about the younger Mr. Dryden," came the surprised response.

"Oh, of course," Jessica said quickly.

BY THE END of the first day, Jessica felt as though she'd put in a forty-hour week. She'd been assigned a small desk in the corner of the room and her own phone. Mrs. Sterling seemed to feel it was her duty to keep Jessica occupied with a multitude of tasks which included taking lunch orders, organizing file cabinets and hand-delivering messages throughout the office.

Just when she was about to think she wouldn't even lay eyes on Evan her first day, he breezed into the office, stopping abruptly when he saw her. He was as tall as Damian, at least six-two, with chestnut hair and dark soulful eyes. To Jessica's way of thinking, it wasn't fair that any one man should be so breathtakingly handsome.

"Julia," he whispered, as though he'd stumbled upon a treasure chest. His eyes suffused with delight. "What are you doing here?"

"It's Jessica," she corrected him, refusing to be offended by his failure to remember her name. "I'm here because I'm working for you now."

"Your brother hired Ms. Kellerman as your new legal assistant," Mrs. Sterling explained.

Evan stepped forward, gripping Jessica's hand in his own. "This must be Christmas in July! Why else would Damian present me with such a rare gift?"

"Christmas in July," Jessica repeated, having a difficult time not laughing. What she'd heard about Evan was true, she decided. He was a flirt, but such a pleasant lighthearted one that it didn't seem to matter. She knew he wasn't serious.

"There are several matters here that need your attention," Mrs. Sterling said stiffly from behind Evan.

"I'll be with you in a few minutes," he said.

"I know you will," Mrs. Sterling said. "Just don't leave before these letters are signed, and while we're at it, there are a few items we need to discuss—when you have the time."

"I promise to get to the letters first thing," he said as if he had no interest beyond studying the young woman who stood before him. "Just put everything on my desk and I'll look through it before I leave."

"You won't forget?"

Evan chuckled. "My, my, how you love to mother me."

"Someone has to look after you," his secretary said, her eyes crinkling above a bright smile.

Jessica watched in amazement as Evan charmed the older woman. Mrs. Sterling had been the picture of cool efficiency until Evan walked in the door. The minute he did she turned into a clucking mother hen. Before Jessica had a chance to analyze this reaction, Evan grinned. "You love me, Mary, and you know it."

"It's just that you've been a bit forgetful of late," Mrs. Sterling said with a concerned frown. She reached for a stack of letters and leafed through them. "It doesn't hurt to offer you a little reminder now and then, does it?"

"I suppose not," Evan said and, taking the letters with him, walked into his office as if he hadn't a care in the world.

"Have you been working on the brief for the Porter Corporation?" Mrs. Sterling asked, following on his heels.

"The Porter Corporation," Evan repeated as if he'd never heard the name before. "It's not due anytime soon, is it?"

"Yes, it is," the secretary said, and Jessica heard a hint of panic in her voice. "First thing Friday morning."

"I'll have it ready by then. What day is this, anyway?"

"Mr. Dryden, you've got to start coming into the office before closing time!"

"Don't you fret. I'll have everything ready the way I always do," he said as he ushered his secretary out the door. He paused when his gaze fell on Jessica and he winked. Then the door closed and Evan disappeared.

Mrs. Sterling shook her head and glanced toward Jessica. "Mr Dryden's been going through some rough times lately," she explained.

"How long has he been without a legal assistant?"

"Quite a while now. He didn't seem to think he'd need one. Damian's cut his work load and, well, things just haven't been the same around here for quite a while."

Jessica was leaving for the day when she happened upon Damian. Looking dignified and businesslike, he was talking to his secretary. A few silver hairs at his temple added a distinguished air. He made a striking figure, and she wondered briefly why he hadn't married. Tagged onto that thought came another. One that took her by surprise. She realized she was *happy* Damian hadn't married.

He must have seen her in his peripheral vision, because he straightened, smiled and walked toward her. "Well, Jessica, how'd your first day go?"

"Really well."

"Mary isn't working you too hard, is she?"

"Oh, no, she's great."

"Mary's one of the best secretaries I've ever worked with. She may be a bit abrupt, but you'll get used to that.'' He was walking with Jessica now, their steps matching, his hands clasped behind his back. Mary was abrupt perhaps, Jessica mused, but not with Evan.

''I'll always be grateful to you for being willing to take a chance on me,'' she said conversationally.

Damian's smile was rueful. ''You may not be thanking me later. My brother can be a handful, but if there was ever someone who could get him back on the straight and narrow, it's you.''

''Me?'' she asked, not understanding.

Damian broke eye contact and looked away. ''Everybody needs to be looked at with wide worshipful eyes now and then, don't you think?''

''Ah...'' Jessica didn't know how to respond. One thing was becoming abundantly clear. Damian hadn't hired her because of her high test scores at business college.

CHAPTER TWO

"YOU ACTUALLY GOT the job?" Cathy Hudson said over the telephone line, her voice raised with astonishment. "You were hired, just like that, by one of the city's most prestigious law firms?"

"It helps to have friends in high places." Jessica was excited about this job, but she felt mildly guilty knowing the only reason she'd been hired was that their families were such good friends. However, Damian had made it plain she'd need to pull her own weight. Jessica was determined to prove herself; she'd be the best legal assistant the firm had ever hired. It was a matter of pride.

"Why is it everything comes so easy for you?" Cathy lamented. "You set your sights on something that would give Norman Vincent Peale second thoughts and—"

"Me? You're the one trying out for a lead in *Guys and Dolls*. Talk about setting your sights high."

"All right, all right," Cathy said with a dramatic sigh, "you've made your point."

"So how did the tryouts go today?"

"I...don't know. It's so hard to tell. I would kill for the part of Adelaide, but then I watch the others, and they're all so good. I came away today thinking it's just a pipe dream. David, the director, is wonderful.

Working with him would be one of the highlights of my career, but I don't dare hope I'll get the part.''

"I have faith in you. You're a natural, Cath." It was true, her friend had a knack for the dramatic, and that had always made their friendship so interesting.

Cathy laughed softly. "How can I fail, when both you and my mother are convinced I'm destined for stardom? Now, before we get off the subject, how did the interview with Damian go?"

"Really well, I think." Damian had dominated her thoughts all afternoon. He'd changed, she decided, or perhaps she was the one who was different. Whichever, she found herself enthralled by the man. The thought of working with him excited her.

"What about the younger brother?"

"Actually I'll be working directly for Evan."

Cathy must have noticed the hesitation in her voice because she asked, "Does that worry you? What's the matter? Do you think you're going to make an idiot of yourself over him—again?"

So much for Jessica's delicate ego. "No way. I was fourteen years old, for heaven's sake."

After she'd hung up, Jessica slipped a CD into the player, choosing an invigorating medley of jazz hits, and set about fixing her dinner. She whipped together a hot chicken-and-spinach salad and stood barefoot in her kitchen, humming along to the music, her heart singing its own melody.

Later that evening, she relaxed with the paper. Despite her best efforts, her thoughts drifted to Damian. The last thing she wanted was to make a fool of herself over another Dryden.

To the best of her knowledge, the source of which was her mother, Damian wasn't currently involved in a relationship. Joyce Kellerman said that Lois Dryden had complained that her elder son didn't take enough time for fun in his life. What Damian needed, Jessica decided now, was to fall in love with a woman who would take his mind off his work. Someone fun. Someone who would make him laugh and enjoy life. Someone who appreciated him.

An hour later, as she was getting ready for bed, Jessica realized she'd spent most of the evening thinking about Damian. Well, quite understandable, she rationalized. After all, he was head of the firm she was working for.

THE FOLLOWING DAY, Evan didn't show up at the office until well after eleven. As she had previously, Mrs. Sterling fussed over him as though he were the prodigal son the moment he waltzed in the door.

"Good morning, Mr. Dryden." Mrs. Sterling gushed, nearly leaping from her chair. "It's a beautiful day, isn't it?"

Evan seemed to need time to think about this. "I hadn't noticed, but you're right, it is a gorgeous day," he said as he reached for his mail and leafed through the envelopes.

He was on his way into his office when he noticed Jessica sitting at her desk. She felt his scrutiny and was pleased that she'd dressed carefully, choosing a smart-looking flowered silk dress with a blue jacket. In her heels, she was nearly as tall as he was.

"Good morning, Mr. Dryden," she offered.

"Evan," he insisted. "You can call Damian Mr. Dryden if you insist, but I'm Evan."

"All right. Good morning, Evan,"

"It is a good morning, isn't it?" he asked, giving her a roguish grin. Jessica couldn't help but respond with a smile of her own. She hadn't noticed it so much the day before, but there were definite changes in the Evan she remembered. He was thinner and his smiles didn't quite reach his eyes. Another thing she couldn't help noticing was the way everyone walked on eggshells around him. Mrs. Sterling had made a point of letting her know Evan's work load had recently been cut, and Damian had said Evan hadn't yet recovered from a broken relationship. It must have been pretty serious, she mused.

"It's been a long time since we've had a chance to talk, hasn't it?" Evan asked, walking over and sitting on the edge of Jessica's desk.

"A very long time," she agreed, praying with all her heart he wouldn't resurrect her girlish antics. It'd been embarrassing enough to have Damian do it.

"I think we should make up for lost opportunities, don't you? Tell you what—I'll treat you to lunch." He checked his watch and seemed surprised at the time. "We'll leave in half an hour. That'll give me enough time to clear whatever's on my desk."

"You want to take me to lunch?" Jessica asked. "Today?"

"It's the least I can do," Evan said with a shrug. "I'll have Mary make reservations."

"But—"

"That's an excellent idea," Mrs. Sterling interjected, clearly pleased.

"I...I've only just started work," Jessica said. "I'd enjoy lunch, perhaps in a week or so, after I've settled into the job." The last thing she wanted was to give Damian the impression she was already slacking in her duties.

Evan pressed his thumb to her chin and gazed deeply into her eyes. "No buts, and no arguments. We're going to lunch and you can fill me in on what you've been doing for the last five or six years."

Mrs. Sterling followed Evan into his office, looking inordinately pleased with the turn of events. She returned a few minutes later, casting a delighted look in Jessica's direction as she picked up her phone and called the restaurant to make reservations. Evan chose Henri's, one of Boston's finest, well-known for its elegant dining. It also happened to be a good fifteen-minute drive from the office, which meant they were going to be out for lunch much longer than usual.

"I doubt we'll be back in an hour if we have lunch at Henri's," Jessica felt obliged to say.

"Don't worry about it. You'll make it up another time, I'm sure."

"But this is only my second day. I don't want to give the wrong impression."

"My dear, Mr. Dryden is your boss. If he wants to take a leisurely lunch with you, don't argue. You should be counting your blessings, instead."

"I know but—"

"From what I understand, you two are old family friends," Mrs. Sterling interrupted. "It's only natural for him to want to personally welcome you into the firm."

It seemed the reservation had barely been made when Evan reappeared. "Are you ready?"

Jessica blinked back her surprise. "Yes, of course, if you'll give me just a moment." She finished typing her notes into the computer, stored the information and pushed back her chair.

Evan took her elbow and told his secretary, "We'll be back in a couple of hours."

They were on their way through the corridor leading to the front of the office when Damian appeared. His gaze shifted from Evan to Jessica.

"Jessica and I are on our way out to lunch," Evan explained. "Do you need me for anything?"

"No. You two go on ahead. I'll talk to you later."

Damian nodded, and it was all Jessica could do not to blurt out that this lunch date hadn't been her idea, but there wasn't the opportunity and she doubted it was necessary anyway. Damian must have known she hadn't invited herself out to lunch. Nevertheless, she didn't want him to think ill of her.

"We'll probably be late getting back," Evan said to his brother, guiding Jessica out of the office.

They arrived at the restaurant by taxi and were seated immediately. The ambience was formal, with soft chamber music playing unobtrusively in the background. The waiters, who dressed like diplomats, were attentive, the tables were well spaced, and the meal was served with a good deal of ceremony.

Evan seemed disinclined to talk about himself, asking her a series of questions about school, her friends and activities. He appeared attentive, but she suspected his thoughts were far removed from her and their lunch. At least he didn't dredge up the past and her infatuation with him. She could have kissed him for that.

After their dishes were cleared away, Evan took out a pad and pen. "I'm going to be working on a civil suit that'll demand a fair amount of research," he told Jessica. His eyes were bright with an enthusiasm she hadn't seen before. "The case involves Earl Kress—you might remember reading about him."

"Of course." The unusual details of the case had filled the local news for weeks. The twenty-year-old former athlete was suing the Spring Valley School District for his education.

Jessica wished she'd brought along a pad and pen herself. She listened, enthralled, as Evan explained the details of the suit. It seemed Earl was a gifted athlete and the key figure in three of the school's biggest sports—football, basketball and track. In order for him to participate in these sports he had to maintain a C average. Unfortunately Earl had a learning disability and had never mastered reading skills. Although he'd graduated from high school and been awarded a full scholarship, he was functionally illiterate.

Evan explained that the school district had pressured Earl's teachers, and they'd been forced to give him passing grades. After he graduated from high school, he went on to college, but a severe knee injury suffered during football training camp effectively ended his career. And within the first two months of school, Earl flunked out.

"That's so unfair," Jessica said when Evan finished. If Damian was concerned about his brother, she thought, then offering Evan this groundbreaking case was sure to take his mind off other things. It would give Evan purpose, a reason to come to work in the morning, the necessary incentive to look past his personal problems.

"There've been a number of similar suits filed in other parts of the country," Evan continued. "I'm going to need you to do extensive research on the outcome of the cases previously tried."

"I'll be happy to help in any way I can."

Evan grinned his appreciation. "I knew I could count on you."

So this was the real reason for their lunch. The case clearly meant a good deal to Evan, and consequently to Jessica. She was grateful for the opportunity to prove herself.

By the time they returned to the office, their lunch hour had stretched to three. It seemed everyone in the office was staring at them, and Jessica felt decidedly uncomfortable.

She walked directly to her desk, keeping her face averted when she passed Damian's office. His door was open, and when he saw her walk by he stood up, called her name and then glanced pointedly at his watch. It was all Jessica could do not to tell him it had been a *business* lunch.

Damian had made it painfully clear that he expected her to do her job. He wasn't paying her to romance his brother during three-hour lunches, and Jessica didn't want him to have that impression. She longed to explain, but she'd look ridiculous doing so in front of Evan. The only thing she could do was stay late that evening in an effort to make up for the time spent over lunch.

Although it was after seven when she started out of the office, a number of others were still there. With her sweater draped over her arm, she was on her way down the long corridor when Damian stopped her.

"Jessica."

"Hello, Damian," she said. He was standing just outside his office.

He relaxed, crossed his arms and asked, "How'd your lunch go with my brother?"

"Very well, but..."

"Yes?" he prompted when she didn't immediately finish.

"I want you to know it was a working lunch," she said, rushing the words in her eagerness to explain. "We discussed the Earl Kress case. I didn't want you to think we'd spent three hours socializing."

"It wouldn't have mattered."

"But it does!" she insisted fervently. "The lawsuit was the reason Evan asked me out. He wasn't interested in renewing an old friendship."

Damian's frown was thoughtful. "Did he seem pleased with the assignment?"

"Very much so," Jessica recalled Mrs. Sterling's saying that "things just haven't been the same around here for quite a while," implying *Evan* hadn't been the same. She wondered if Damian realized the extent of his brother's unhappiness.

Damian grinned; Jessica had the feeling he didn't do that often, which was a shame. The grooves in his cheeks and the sparkle in his gray eyes were very attractive. "I thought he might need a change of pace. Did you two have a chance to talk about old times?"

This was a casual way of asking if she'd noticed the changes in his brother, Jessica guessed. "A little. Evan really was hurt, wasn't he?"

Damian nodded. "Generally he disguises it, but I wondered if you'd detect the changes in him."

"I couldn't help noticing." She'd seen it almost from the first moment. Even though she hadn't seen Evan for years she could see how hard he was struggling to hide his misery. No wonder his parents and brother were so concerned.

Damian glanced at his watch and arched his brows. "It's late. We'll talk again some other time. Good night, Jessica."

"Good night, Damian."

As she waited for a train in the subway station, Jessica at last understood what Damian had meant when he'd told her that everyone needed to be looked at with wide worshipful eyes sometimes. It made perfect sense now that she thought about it. Damian still viewed her as that teenage girl infatuated with his younger brother. If ever there was a time that Evan needed a woman to idolize him, it was now. She'd been hired, not for her legal skills, but to help his brother forget the woman he'd loved and lost. Damian was looking to her to heal Evan's pain.

THE FOLLOWING MORNING around ten, Evan, his smile bright enough to rival the sun, breezed into the office and presented Jessica with a bouquet of a dozen bloodred roses. Their perfume filled the room.

Jessica was speechless. "For me?" The flowers took her completely by surprise. Mrs. Sterling, too, from the look the secretary cast her.

"I need a favor," Evan said, leaning against the edge of her desk, his face scant inches from her own.

"Of course." She was holding the flowers against her like a beauty queen, inhaling their heavenly scent.

Evan reached into his jacket pocket and withdrew a folded sheet of yellow paper. "I need you to do some last-minute research for me."

"Certainly."

"There're some statutes I need you to look up and report back to me on as soon as possible. This stuff is as dry as old bones—I'm sorry about that."

"Don't worry about it." Jessica looked at the items Evan wanted her to research and her heart sank at the number. "How soon do you need this?"

"Yesterday," was his frank reply.

Mrs. Sterling made a small tsk-tsk sound in the background, which made Jessica smile. Evan's eyes twinkled and he whispered, "There's nothing worse than a woman who can't let 'I told you so' pass. Remember that, Jessica."

"I will," she said with a small laugh. "I'd best get started. I'll have the information for you before I leave tonight."

"Good girl."

Mrs. Sterling produced a vase for the roses, and after setting them on the edge of her desk Jessica got down to work. She ensconced herself in the library and kept at her research straight through the lunch hour. She didn't notice the time until it was after three, when her stomach rumbled in protest. Even then she didn't take the time to sit down to eat, but grabbed an apple and munched on it while she continued to search for the required data.

The next time she looked up, the clock on the wall said seven forty-five. She'd heard the others leave, but that seemed like only minutes ago. She stood up and, placing her hand at the base of her spine, arched her stiff back and breathed in deeply.

Her eyes felt tired and her back sore as she carried her paperwork into the office. She stopped, surprised to find the room dark. She flicked on the lights and looked around, certain Evan had left a note for her.

He hadn't.

Picking up one of the roses, she held it to her nose and closed her eyes as she tried to battle down the weariness—and the disappointment.

"Jessica, what are you doing here?"

"Damian." She could ask the same question of him.

"It's nearly eight o'clock."

"I know." She rotated her overworked shoulders. "I guess time got away from me."

"So I see. I had some reading I was catching up on, but I assumed I was here alone. There was no reason for you to stay this late."

She glanced toward Evan's office. "What time did Evan leave?" she asked casually, not wanting him to know how abused she felt.

"A couple of hours ago. Why?"

"He said he needed this information right away." She'd been in a frenzy attempting to finish the task as quickly as possible. She'd assumed he would wait until she'd collected the data he seemed to need so desperately.

"I believe he had a dinner engagement," Damian explained.

"I see," she muttered. In other words, he'd cheerfully abandoned her.

"You sound angry," Damian said.

"I am. I worked through my lunch hour getting this stuff for him." And dinner hour, too, she thought, feeling even angrier. She realized too late that she probably also sounded jealous.

"I'm sorry, Jessica."

Evan's thoughtlessness wasn't Damian's fault and she said so, then asked bluntly, "Is there anything to eat around here?" She blinked back unexpected tears. Hunger always had a strange effect on her emotions, but it was embarrassing, and she tried not to let Damian see.

"You mean you haven't eaten since lunch?"

"Not since breakfast, unless you count an apple, and if I don't eat soon I'm going to cry and you really wouldn't want to witness that." The words rushed out and she felt a sniffle coming on. "Never mind," she muttered, turning away from him. She wiped her nose with her forearm and returned to the library. Several ponderous law volumes were spread open across the tables. She closed them and began lugging them back to the shelves.

"I found a package of soda crackers," Damian said, coming into the room.

"Thanks," she said, ripping away the clear plastic wrapper and sniffling again. "I'm sorry, I don't mean to act like this." She ate a cracker quickly and managed to hold back a sob. "Don't look so concerned. I just needed to eat."

"Let me take you to dinner." Damian lifted a couple of the volumes and replaced them for her.

"That isn't necessary." A second cracker had made its way into her mouth and she was beginning to feel more like herself.

"We owe you that much," Damian countered. "Besides, I'm half-starved myself."

"The least he could have done was waited," Jessica fumed.

Ignoring her comment Damian suggested a popular seafood restaurant nearby.

"He made it sound like it was a matter of life and death, and then he doesn't even bother to tell me he's leaving," she continued to fume. "You're right," she said as Damian cupped her elbow and led her out the door. "Evan *has* changed."

Damian didn't respond to this comment either.

They walked the three blocks to the restaurant. It wasn't too crowded, and they were given immediate seating at a wooden table near one of the windows. Even better, the waitress brought hot bread and chowder no more than a minute after it was ordered. Damian must be a regular here to get such service, Jessica thought, her good mood restored now that her stomach had something warm and filling.

"This is excellent," she said. "Thank you." She sighed in contentment as she spooned up the last of her chowder.

Grinning, he finished his own soup, then reached for another piece of bread.

"What's so funny?" she demanded. How like a man to keep something humorous to himself and then feel superior about it.

"I think I might just have averted a lawsuit. Can't you hear it? 'Woman Sues Boss over Lost Meals.'"

"I'd get a huge settlement." The corners of her mouth twitched with a smile. Her eyes met Damian's and soon their amusement had blossomed into full-blown grins.

He had very nice eyes, Jessica mused. They were a dark gray and revealed his keen intelligence, his sharp insight. She wanted to clear away any lingering misconception he had about her and Evan, but she couldn't think of a way to do it without sounding as if she was jealous of whatever person Evan spent his personal time with.

Jessica wondered what Damian saw when he looked at her. Did he see the woman she'd become, or did he view her as the pesky kid next door who'd adamantly declared that his younger brother was her destiny?

The waitress arrived then with their main courses. Damian had ordered oysters and Jessica baked cod, which was delicious. By the time they'd finished, she felt completely restored.

"I said some things I shouldn't have back at the office," Jessica began, feeling self-conscious now but eager to explain. "You see—"

"You'd worked far longer than necessary and were starving to boot," he interrupted. "Don't worry about it."

"I just wanted to be sure I hadn't provoked you into firing me."

"It'll take more than a demand for food to do that," he assured her, hardly disguising his amusement.

The June sky was dark and overcast and the temperature cooler as they came down the stairs and into the street. "It looks like rain," Damian said. No sooner had he spoken when fat raindrops began to fall. Taking Jessica by the elbow, he raced across the street. Neither had thought to bring an umbrella.

"Here," Damian said, running toward an alcove in front of a bookstore. The business had closed hours earlier, but the covered entrance was a good place to wait out the cloudburst. Jessica was breathless by the time they stopped. A chill raced over her and she rubbed her arms vigorously.

Damian's much larger hands replaced hers, then he stopped and peeled off his jacket, draping it over her shoulders.

"Damian, I'm fine," she protested, fearing he'd catch a chill himself.

"You're shivering."

The warmth of his coat was more welcome than she cared to admit. No doubt about it, Damian was a gentleman to the very core.

The downpour lasted a good ten minutes. Jessica was surprised at how quickly the time passed. When the storm dwindled to a drizzle and eventually stopped, Jessica discovered she was almost sorry. She was talking books with Damian and discovered they both shared an interest in murder mysteries. Damian was as well-read as she was, and they tossed titles and authors' names back and forth without a pause.

"Did you drive to work this morning?" he asked.

She shook her head. She'd taken the subway.

"I'll give you a lift home, then."

"Really, Damian, that isn't necessary. I don't mind using public transit."

"*I* mind," he said in a voice that brooked no argument. "It's too late for you to be out on the streets alone."

How sweet of him to worry about her, she thought. "But I already have enough to thank you for."

"What do you mean?"

"I was just thinking—I seem to be continually in your debt. You've got a heart of gold."

He chuckled. "Hardly, little Jessica."

"You hired me without any real job experience, then you fed me dinner, and now you're driving me home."

"It's the least I can do."

They returned to the office building, walking directly to the underground parking garage. Damian opened the car door for her and she nestled back in the leather seat.

One thing she'd learned during their time together was the fact that Damian was protective of his younger brother, though she doubted Evan appreciated that.

"You're worried about him, aren't you?" she asked, without clarifying her question. Damian knew who she was talking about.

"Yeah," he admitted.

"Evan's the real reason you hired me, isn't he? You think I might be able to help him through this... difficult time." It wasn't a responsibility she welcomed or wanted. She was about to explain that when she noticed the way his mouth quirked into an amused smile.

Instead, she told him sharply, "I'm not a silly fourteen-year-old infatuated with an older man. What I felt for your brother was just a crush. It was over years ago." That was the simple truth.

His shrug was noncommittal.

"Nevertheless," she forged on, "you hired me because of Evan?"

It took Damian a long time to answer. "Sometimes I wonder," he finally said. "Sometimes I wonder."

CHAPTER THREE

JESSICA ARRIVED EARLY the following morning, hoping to have an opportunity to thank Damian again for dinner and more importantly to let him know how much she'd enjoyed the time they'd shared. But when she passed his office, the door was closed and his secretary was searching urgently through a file drawer. It didn't look like the time to pop in unannounced.

Not surprisingly, Evan was nowhere to be seen. Mrs. Sterling arrived ten minutes after Jessica, greeting her with a small approving smile, and set about sorting through the mail.

Jessica spent the first part of the morning organizing the material she'd researched the day before and typing up her notes. That way, Evan wouldn't be forced to waste time deciphering her hasty scrawl.

She'd just completed printing out the results when a breathless Evan entered the office. From the look of him, he'd raced all the way up from the parking garage. Briefcase in hand, he marched up to her desk.

"Do you have those notes ready?" he asked, reaching for the file before Jessica had a chance to present it. She stood up, intending to discuss a number of points with him, but he brushed past her and hurried into his office without a word. She would have followed him, but he closed the door.

Jessica was taken aback; unsure of what to do, she looked at Mrs. Sterling. The secretary sighed and shrugged. "Working for Mr. Dryden can be a real trial," she muttered, then grinned and added, "No pun intended."

No sooner had Mrs. Sterling finished chuckling over her own little joke than Evan reappeared, looking composed and confident. He'd removed his raincoat and was leafing casually through the file. He looked over at Jessica and his face relaxed into a broad smile.

"You're an angel," he said, kissing her cheek as he walked past. Jessica had seen him kiss Mrs. Sterling in the same affectionate way.

"I'll be in a meeting with Damian this morning," Evan announced on his way out the door.

As the morning progressed, Jessica found herself wondering exactly what her role in the office was. Although Evan had recently been assigned the Earl Kress case, his work load had been light in the past few months. Now that she'd finished the research project, there was barely enough to keep her busy.

From various bits and pieces, Jessica had learned that Evan's interest in corporate law had waned recently. Surely Damian hadn't hired her expecting miracles! Since he was so closemouthed about Evan's troubles, Jessica wondered if Mrs. Sterling could fill in some details. She didn't want to be obvious about asking, which could prove tricky since the woman was so clearly devoted to her employer.

"That Evan's a real charmer, isn't he?" Jessica began conversationally.

"He always could charm the birds right out the trees," Mrs. Sterling answered proudly.

"He's different now from the way I remember him. More...intense."

Evan's secretary nodded and muttered, "I'd like to shoot that woman."

Jessica's heart leapt with excitement. "What woman?" she asked, hoping to hide her eagerness. She was about to learn what had happened to change Evan so drastically from the man she'd known.

Mrs. Sterling glanced up, as if surprised that Jessica had heard her mumbling. "Oh...it's nothing."

"But it *must* be something. Evan isn't anything like he was a few years back. Oh, he's charming and sweet, but there's an edge to him now. A sharpness, I guess. Something I can't put my finger on." She looked expectantly at the other woman.

"That's true enough," Mrs. Sterling reluctantly conceded.

"You say a woman's responsible for the changes in Evan?"

"Isn't it always a woman?"

"What happened?" Might as well try a more direct approach, Jessica thought. Tact wasn't getting her anywhere.

"It's a pity, a real pity."

"Yes, Evan just isn't the same," Jessica said, hoping to encourage the other woman to continue.

"It shouldn't come as any surprise, really. Yet it does, Mr. Dryden being the charmer he is. Plain and simple, he fell in love with someone who didn't feel the same way about him." Then she clamped her mouth closed as though she'd already said far more than she should—far more than was circumspect for a secretary to say about her boss.

But this much she already knew. What she was looking for were the particulars. Who was this woman who'd hurt Evan so badly? Her back stiffened at the thought of someone rejecting him. The man she'd worshiped from afar during her tumultuous teenage years. Whoever this woman was, Jessica decided, she was a fool.

About eleven Evan walked into the office. He smiled as he strolled past Mrs. Sterling's desk to hers. "The research you did was wonderful, Jessica. Thank you."

His appreciation caught her off guard. She wondered if Damian had said something to him and was momentarily speechless.

"I appreciate the effort that went into your report," he continued. "I'm very pleased by the quality of your work."

"I . . . I was happy to do it. That's my . . . my job." The words stumbled off the end of her tongue. Jessica was amazed that his praise could fluster her so. She was embarrassed now by the way she'd overreacted last night when she'd learned he'd left the office. It was her own fault for not taking time to eat lunch. Evan's disappearance wouldn't have bothered her in the least if she had. . . .

"Damian said you were here till almost eight."

So Damian *had* mentioned that. "As I said earlier, I was only doing my job."

"Mom and Dad are having a barbecue this weekend," Evan continued, "Saturday, around four. I'd like you to attend it with me."

His invitation threw her. She wasn't sure what to say. Although she hadn't had a lot of work experience, she knew that dating the boss could lead to problems.

"This shouldn't be a difficult decision," Evan said, grinning.

His pride had already suffered one blow, and Jessica discovered she was unwilling to deliver a second, no matter how slight. "I'd enjoy that very much," she said. "Thank you for thinking of me."

He smiled affectionately. "You always were a sweet thing."

As a teenager, Jessica's daydreams had been filled with such scenarios. She'd close her eyes and pretend Evan had asked her out. Now her dream had come true, but Jessica was left wishing it had been Damian issuing the invitation, instead of his brother.

"I'll pick you up. You are living in the city, aren't you?"

Jessica nodded. "Wouldn't it be simpler if we met at the party? As it happens, I'm spending the weekend with my parents, and I can walk over with them."

Evan seemed a bit surprised by her suggestion. "You're sure?"

"Positive."

"Then that'll be fine. I'll look forward to seeing you there."

There'd been a time in her life when she would have gladly walked across a bed of hot coals to attend a party with Evan. Any party. Anywhere. Hadn't Damian been counting on that when he hired her—even if he claimed to know she was long over her crush?

"The festivity's in honor of some dignitary," Evan went on. "Mom's worked herself into a tizzy for the event. I can guarantee this will be the most elaborate barbecue Boston has ever seen. The last I heard, Mom hired a country-and-western band.''

''It sounds like fun.''

''Considering all the effort that's going into it, I'm sure it will be. You can do the two-step, can't you, sweet Jessica?''

''Of course.'' How easy it was to stretch the truth. In fact, she'd only done the two-step once or twice before. ''Well, I'm pretty rusty,'' she amended.

''Me, too. We'll leave the fancy footwork to Damian.''

Damian, she thought with a sigh. There was definitely something wrong with her, something psychological, something rooted deep in her childhood, she guessed, if she could agree to date one brother while longing for the other.

The hours flew by and before Jessica knew it, the workday had come to an end. Mrs. Sterling had just stepped out of the office when Damian strolled casually in.

''Evan's left for the day,'' Jessica said, a little flustered to find him standing in front of her desk. Especially since she'd again been thinking how much she'd have preferred to attend the family barbecue with *him*.

''I'm not here to see my brother.''

''Mrs. Sterling will be right back.''

''I came to see you,'' Damian explained, his eyes dark and intense as they settled on her.

Jessica tensed. Did he have some complaint with her work?

''Don't look so worried. I came to tell you my parents are holding a party this weekend. A barbecue.''

"Yes, I know. Evan mentioned it earlier."

Jessica swore Damian's eyes brightened with interest. He crossed his arms and leaned against her desk. "What did he say about it?"

"Not much. Apparently it's in honor of some dignitary."

"I see." He hesitated as if he was unsure, which Jessica knew was completely out of character for Damian. "I was wondering..." he began, then straightened and buried his hands deep in his pants pockets. "Would you like to come to the party with me?"

Her shoulders sagged as she opened her mouth to explain that Evan had already invited her, but before she could respond, Damian added, "I realize it's short notice, but I didn't hear the details myself until this morning." A hint of a smile turned up the corners of his mouth. "Mother phoned, wanting to be sure I'd be there. She seems to be taking her duties very seriously."

"Ah..."

"There's a problem," he guessed.

She nodded glumly. "Evan's already invited me to the party—as his date." She wanted to tell Damian she'd much prefer to attend with him, but she couldn't. "I'm sorry," she added.

"He did?" Instead of looking displeased at this turn of events, Damian sounded positively delighted. "Don't be sorry."

His reaction annoyed her.

"It isn't like a real date," she said, wanting to make that clear. "At least, that wasn't the impression Evan gave me. The invitation was his way of thanking me for working so hard on the research project."

"My brother wouldn't invite you if he wasn't interested in your company," Damian insisted. "Besides, I wouldn't want my brother to think I was cutting in on his territory."

His territory.

Damian must have guessed her feelings, because he said, "Evan asked you first."

He was right about that, she thought, but little else.

Damian turned away, and it suddenly became important to Jessica to explain herself. "I don't think you should put much stock in Evan's invitation. It really *was* just a way of thanking me."

"It's a start, though, don't you think?" Damian said over his shoulder. "A good start, at that." He left her then before she could say anything more.

Jessica was upset, and it wasn't until she got home that she figured out why. Damian hadn't invited her to the party out of any real desire for her company. He'd assumed that Evan hadn't asked her—and he was looking for an opportunity to throw her and his brother together socially.

JESSICA ARRIVED at her parents' house early Saturday afternoon, after spending all morning shopping for the perfect outfit. Cathy had come along to offer encouragement and advice.

She might not be attending the barbecue with Damian, but when she showed up looking like a movie star, he'd wish she was. This was her mission, plain and simple.

Evan had casually mentioned the country-and-western band, but he'd also said the barbecue was in honor of some dignitary. These somewhat contradictory snippets of information served to confuse her about how to dress. Nothing in her closet seemed suitable, but then little in the shops did, either.

In one outfit she resembled Annie Oakley, and in another Jackie Kennedy. There didn't seem to be much of a middle ground—until she found a long denim skirt, a red shirt decorated with rainbow-colored fringe sewn about the yoke and white cowboy boots. A white silk scarf tied around her neck lent a touch of elegance.

Her mother's eyes widened with approval when Jessica modeled the outfit. "I wish now I'd gone shopping, too, and bought something new myself. You look great."

"Thanks." Her mother's praise gave Jessica confidence. Cathy, who tended to dress like a character in a sci-fi movie, had also said she looked great, but Jessica wasn't sure she trusted her friend's fashion sense.

"It was so sweet of Evan to include you," Joyce Kellerman went on to say. "Not that I'm surprised, his being your boss and all. Life is certainly full of little twists and turns, isn't it?

"It sure is," Jessica said without elaborating.

"I'm thrilled that you're working with Evan."

"He's a nice person."

"He's *wonderful.* It's always been my dream, I know it's silly, but well, we're such good friends with the Drydens... I've hoped you'd grow up to marry one of Lois's boys."

"Whatever you do," Jessica said quickly, "don't say that in front of Damian or Evan."

"Why not, dear?"

"Mom, it'd embarrass me to death!"

"But you were so keen on Evan a few years back, and I thought... I hoped..."

"Mother, I was only fourteen!" Her old infatuation with Evan was turning into the proverbial albatross around her neck—thanks to Damian and her mother. If it wasn't for them, the whole thing would have been forgotten by now.

"You'll make a beautiful bride," her mother said, adding the finishing touches to her own outfit. Suddenly she changed the subject. "Lois has worried herself sick over this silly barbecue."

"But why?" Mrs. Dryden had thrown a hundred parties more elaborate than this.

Her mother sat on the bed and leaned back on her hands. "I don't suppose there's any reason to keep it a secret. Walter's been approached about running for the Senate."

Walter Dryden had been active in community affairs for years. Although he'd never held public office, he'd often managed the successful campaigns of others. He'd taken an early retirement from the law firm, and, from what Jessica understood, had grown restless with inactivity. Running for office would doubtless come as a welcome challenge.

"Has he decided he's going to run?"

"Your father and I think so. He hasn't declared his candidacy yet, but we're confident he will. He's testing the waters with this barbecue tonight. Several people from the political arena will be present. This is probably the most important party of Lois's marriage. Little wonder she's a nervous wreck.''

Even before Jessica and her parents arrived for the barbecue, the pungent smells of tomato sauce, spices and roasting meat mingled with the afternoon sunshine and drifted over the fence.

As they were greeted at the front door, Jessica was reminded, by the way Lois hugged her mother, what very good friends the two women were. Their friendship had spanned twenty years, and they were like sisters. Jessica felt the same way about Cathy. They'd met in college, where they'd been roommates for three years.

When Jessica didn't immediately see Evan or Damian, she wandered outside. A series of round tables decorated in red checked tablecloths were scattered across the lush expanse of lawn. The day was perfect, warm but not hot, and the sky was cloudless. A soft breeze ruffled the leaves of the large shade trees that lined the property. This was New England summer at its best. The smells of food were heavenly, too, reminding her how hungry she was. Shopping and preparing for the party hadn't left time for lunch.

Several dozen guests had arrived, and Jessica scanned the crowd. She spotted Evan standing next to a lovely blonde in a chic white fringed dress with a turquoise belt and silver buckle. Jessica didn't recognize the woman, and a few discreet inquiries got her nowhere. She became all the more curious. She attempted to make her way to Evan, since she was officially his date, but in actuality, she was seeking an introduction to the lovely blonde. Perhaps this was Evan's new romantic interest, she thought hopefully.

But before she could reach Evan, she was waylaid by some family friends. Most of the Drydens' guests were older people, established names Jessica had known or heard all her life.

"Hello, Jessica," Damian said from behind her. She turned to find him in the sort of suit he wore at the office. He'd made an attempt to dress to the theme with a black Stetson, which, Jessica thought, looked entirely out of place on his very Bostonian head.

His eyes glimmered with appreciation. "You look—" he hesitated as though he didn't know what to say "—good."

Jessica wagered that it wasn't often Damian was at a loss for words. It lifted her spirits considerably.

"I imagine you're wondering who that blonde is, the one draping herself all over Evan," he suggested casually.

Jessica pretended she was, although she couldn't help being grateful to this unknown woman for keeping Evan occupied. Otherwise he might feel obliged to pay attention to her, and she'd much rather spend her time with Damian.

"Who is she?" Jessica asked, playing his game.

"Do I detect a small hint of jealousy?"

"Of course not." The question irritated her.

"That's Romilda Sidonie."

"Who?"

"The European dignitary's daughter."

That explained it. Naturally Evan considered it his duty to make Romilda feel welcome. Jessica was pleased to see him apparently enjoying himself.

"Would you like me to introduce you?" Damian asked.

"No," Jessica said, noticing Evan and Romilda moving toward the dance area. "Evan's having a good time. I don't see any reason to interrupt him."

"You're his date."

"But only because you prompted him into asking me."

Damian's eyes narrowed. "What makes you say that?"

"I'm not completely naive, you know. I think the reason you came into my office to invite me was that you didn't think Evan had—you wanted to make sure the two of us were together in a social situation so you could see what happened. Am I right?"

He joined his hands behind his back and took two small steps away, then turned to face her again. She saw a hint of a smile in his eyes. "If you're right—though I'm not saying you are—I'd never admit it."

"You must wreak havoc on a jury."

"That's what my clients pay me for."

Jessica looked toward the dance area again and couldn't see Evan and the European woman. When she glanced over at the picnic area, she found the pair sitting at a table beneath a large elm tree munching on barbecue sandwiches.

"She's lovely," Jessica murmured, watching the couple. "No wonder Evan's forgotten me."

"Romilda may be lovely, but so are you," Damian returned quickly, then looked as if he regretted speaking.

"Thank you."

"I shouldn't have said that."

"Why not? That makes me think you didn't mean it."

"I shouldn't be the one saying such things to you," Damian replied. "You're Evan's date."

"He seems to have forgotten, which is just as well. I'd rather spend my time with you."

"With me?" Damian repeated, sounding appalled by the mere suggestion. "Have you eaten?" he asked hurriedly. They were standing next to the dessert table. It was laden with an enormous chocolate cake decorated with fresh strawberries, a lemon torte that would have tempted a saint and a fresh blueberry cobbler, which Jessica knew from years past was the caterer's specialty.

"I'm not hungry just yet," she said, thinking Damian might have used her desire to eat as an excuse to squire her away to one of the tables and conveniently leave her.

Damian eyed her speculatively. "You're sure about that? I'd hate to see a repeat of what happened the other night."

"Well, yes, I guess I will have a bite…but may I sit with you?"

"If you insist."

She did. Damian handed her a plate. Together they walked along the buffet table. Jessica helped herself to potato salad, baked beans and a generous rack of spareribs.

The band started to play a popular tune, and her foot tapping to the beat, Jessica enjoyed the culinary feast. She was content to sit on the sidelines. Evan seemed to have forgotten her, but far from being offended, she felt only a sense of relief.

Damian's invitation to dance came as a surprise. "Why do you want to dance with me?" she asked. She had a sneaking suspicion it somehow involved his brother.

"Do I need a reason?"

Jessica hesitated, then nodded. "If you're thinking it's a way to get Evan to notice me, then I'd rather sit out."

"What if I said it was because I wanted to see how you felt in my arms?"

Her heart gave a flutter. "Then I'd agree." She met his gaze directly. "So, what's it to be, Damian?"

He took a long time deciding, much longer than should have been necessary. Slowly he pushed back his chair and stood. "Why don't we find out together," he suggested, leading her by the hand toward the farthest reaches of the dance area.

The party was in full swing by now, with a good number of couples two-stepping around the area. When several old family friends stopped to chat with Jessica and Damian as they made their way toward the other dancers, Jessica could sense Damian's impatience.

They reached the outskirts of the crowd, and Damian turned Jessica in his arms. They fit together nicely, thigh to thigh, hip to hip. Damian was an excellent dancer, his steps easy to follow, his movements smooth and assured. He held her loosely about the waist and gazed down at her as if they'd been dancing together all their lives.

"You're good at this." Her surprise must have been obvious, because he threw back his head and laughed. It was the first time she could ever remember hearing Damian really laugh.

"That amazes you, doesn't it?" he said.

"Yes." It was pointless to deny it. She was discovering that Damian was full of surprises. Just then Jessica felt someone brush against her. She turned to see Evan, partnered with the dignitary's daughter.

"Well, well, if it isn't Damian and Jessica." Evan said with a smile, not sounding jealous in the least.

It hadn't taken long to attract Evan's attention, and Jessica groaned inwardly, wondering if Damian had planned it this way.

"You haven't met Romilda, have you?" Evan murmured. Without waiting for a response, he made the introductions.

Jessica could see that the blonde had fallen under Evan's spell, just like most women did when he'd decided to charm them. His magnetism was lethal. Jessica nearly felt sorry for the unsuspecting woman. Evan did have a bit of a reputation as a playboy.

The two couples moved off to get something to drink. They were making small talk and sipping punch when Damian suddenly asked Romilda to dance. The woman glanced anxiously at Evan, obviously reluctant to leave him. Jessica smiled softly to herself, recognizing Damian's ploy. He'd all but thrown her and Evan together.

Damian and Romilda joined the throng of dancers. "It's a wonderful party," Jessica said to Evan. "I've been having a good time."

"Glad to hear it," Evan commented distractedly, his eyes following the other couple. "Shall we?" he asked, holding out his hand to her.

It became apparent as they moved into the dancing area that Evan was more interested in keeping an eye on Romilda than dancing with Jessica. She and Evan made polite conversation, but his attention wandered as often as her own. The dance couldn't end soon enough for either of them.

When it did, she was grateful Damian and Romilda were on the far side of the dance area, because she needed time and space to put order to her thoughts. When the number ended, Evan was corralled by an older couple who wanted to talk to him privately. He cast Jessica an apologetic look and moved away.

She strolled to the far reaches of the property, near the fence that bordered her parents' home. A white footbridge spanned a good-size pond. She stood in the middle of the bridge, dropping small rocks into the still water and watching the ripples radiate to the shore one after another.

Thus absorbed, she didn't hear Damian approach and was startled to hear him speak. "I wondered if I'd find you here," he said.

"I used to come here a lot when I was growing up," Jessica admitted. "I guess you could have charged me with trespassing."

"Not too likely."

"I know, that's why I used to come. It was so peaceful. So safe." A duck glided past, disturbing the water in the pond, and Jessica wished she'd thought to bring some bread crumbs. The ducks had often been beneficiaries of her trips here.

Damian was silent for a moment, then he said, "You're discouraged, aren't you?"

"About what?"

"It's over, you know," Damian assured her softly. "It was over a long time ago—more than six months now. I thought Evan would get over her, but I was wrong.''

Oh, dear, Jessica thought. Apparently Damian believed she was here at the pond brooding about Evan, when in fact nothing could have been farther from the truth. She'd been standing on the bridge thinking about her relationship with Damian.

"Who was she?" Jessica was still curious.

"Someone he met on a beach. No name the family had ever heard of before, not that it mattered. Mary Jo Summerhill."

"What happened."

"I don't think anyone really knows for sure. Whatever it was devastated Evan. He hasn't been the same since. My brother isn't one to burden others with his problems. He's like that duck down there on the pond—everything seems to roll off him like water. He'd been in and out of a dozen relationships, and I assumed he was never going to really fall for any woman, but I was wrong."

"You haven't a clue what happened between him and Mary Jo?"

"No. He changed abruptly after the breakup, started working odd hours. But his heart clearly wasn't in it, so I cut back his work load. That helped for a time, but now I'm not sure it was the right thing to do. I've never seen him more miserable."

"Have you tried to talk to him?"

"A dozen times," Damian admitted, "but it hasn't helped. If anything, he's resented my prying. This broken relationship seems to have cut him more deeply than he's willing to admit."

"He'll get over her," Jessica said reassuringly. "It just takes time."

"I thought so, too." Damian shrugged. "But now I wonder. It's been more than six months." He paused, gazing down at the water. "He needs you, Jessica. You might be the only one able to reach him."

"Me?"

"I knew the minute Dad mentioned you were coming in to apply for a job that you could well be the answer to our prayers." She started to say something, but Damian wouldn't let her. "You're just going to need a lot of patience."

Jessica sighed in frustration. "If I'm going to need patience, it's with *you*. You and your family seem to think I'm still a kid with a crush on Evan."

Damian's eyes darkened. "All right, all right, I didn't mean to offend you. You're old enough to make up your own mind."

"Thank you for that," she said. Turning away from him, she rested her hands on the railing and stared into the serene waters below. "I remember once when I was about six coming to this bridge and crying my eyes out," she murmured.

"What hurt you so badly then?"

"You," she said, turning and jabbing a finger at his chest.

"Me?" Jessica had never seen such an expression of outraged innocence. "What did I do?" Damian demanded.

"Your father was taking you and Evan to the roller coaster at Cannon Beach. My dad was out of town on business, and our mothers were taking the shopping cure. They weren't keen on having to drag me along, and I can't remember who, but one of them suggested I go to the carnival with you and Evan."

"And I didn't want you with us," Damian finished for her.

"Not that I blame you. No fifteen-year-old wants a six-year-old girl tagging along."

Damian chuckled. "Times change, don't they?"

Her mother had said the same thing earlier. *Indeed, times do change.*

To Jessica's astonishment, Damian reached for her hand. He linked their fingers and tugged her off the bridge. "Where are we going?" she protested. He looked at her in surprise, as though she hadn't already guessed. "Where else? The beach. From what I understand the same roller coaster is still running. The party here is starting to wind down, and I don't think we'll be missed, do you?"

She couldn't help but agree.

CHAPTER FOUR

CARRYING A STICKY BALL of pink cotton candy in one hand and a purple stuffed elephant under the other, Jessica strolled leisurely with Damian down the long pier. The tinny music of the merry-go-round played behind them, mingling with children's laughter. The scent of the bay and fresh popcorn swirled around them like smoke from a cooling fire. The night was perfect. The sun had set, and clusters of bright stars blinked approvingly down on them.

"I don't think I've ever enjoyed myself more," Jessica said to Damian. She tipped the cotton-candy cone toward him and he helped himself to a handful. Taking another bite herself, she savored the way the sugary sweetness melted on her tongue.

"We still haven't gone on the roller coaster," Damian reminded her.

"That's because you spent all that time trying to win that silly stuffed elephant." She hugged it against her, belying her words.

"Are you game?" Damian asked, looking toward the huge steel structure.

Jessica hedged. "I . . . I don't know if that's such a good idea after all the junk we've eaten."

"Trust me." He looped his arm through hers and pulled her along, not giving her a chance to protest.

"Great, first you fill me up with popcorn and cotton candy, then you insist on dragging me onto one of the biggest roller coasters in the country. That's not smart, Damian, not smart at all."

The crowds were thicker than ever, and Damian reached for her hand as he led her toward the ride. The line was long, and the wait was sure to be at least thirty minutes. A list of possible arguments crowded Jessica's mind, but she knew it wouldn't do any good. The determined set of Damian's jaw told her that much.

"What am I supposed to do with the elephant?" she asked, clinging to it tightly, as they edged closer.

"Hold it."

"If I'm holding the elephant, who's going to hold me?"

"I will," he assured her calmly. "Stop looking so worried."

"I should tell you, Damian Dryden, the last time I rode on this thing I had a near-death experience. I don't suppose you know when this ride had a safety inspection."

"Thursday."

"You don't *know* that!"

He laughed, seeming to enjoy her unease. "True, but it sounded good. Listen, this roller coaster has been running for twenty years without a single mishap. Well, there was that one time..."

"Damian!"

"I was joking."

"Don't tease," Jessica muttered furiously. She flattened her palm against her stomach and sighed loudly. "My stomach doesn't feel right."

"You won't be sick."

"How can you be sure?"

"Experience. Anticipation's the worst part. The ride itself is fun. The only problem is that it doesn't last long enough. The whole thing is over in no time."

For all her complaining, as the minutes passed, Jessica found herself beginning to anticipate their turn. At last the silver cars came to an abrupt halt right in front of them.

"Just promise me you won't fling your arms up in the air in that bizarre descent ritual," Jessica murmured as the bar fell into place, securing them in the seat.

"I wouldn't dream of it," Damian said, "not when I promised to hold on to you."

Jessica colored slightly, but didn't respond. She dared not look down. Heights were something she generally avoided, which meant she was trapped into closing her eyes. The stuffed elephant was cradled in her arms, much the same way Damian was cradling her.

The cars slowly made their ascent, chugging up the steep incline, making a straining noise as if the weight was too much to bear. The line of cars topped the peak and started its rapid descent. A scream of excitement froze in her throat as they plummeted downward. Damian's arm tightened around her shoulders. Her free hand gripped his, her nails digging into his fingers, but if she was hurting him, he gave no indication. Just when it seemed they were about to break the sound barrier, they started up another steep grade, which slowed the momentum, but once they reached the top they were cast on a crazy twisting, turning journey that left her stomach far behind. Her eyes were closed so tightly her face ached.

When at last they rolled to a halt, Jessica's shoulders surged forward, righted and then sagged with a twinge of disappointment as she realized the ride was over.

"Well?" Damian asked, taking her hand to help her climb out of the cramped car. "Did you or did you not have fun?"

Her legs felt a little shaky once she started walking. "Give me a minute—I don't know what I'm feeling." Confessing he'd been right was too much to ask.

Damian laughed. "Admit it. Don't be shy. It was fun, wasn't it?"

"Yes," Jessica said with ill grace.

Damian laughed again and tucked his arm around her waist. His action seemed so natural, especially since it was evident that her knees had yet to right themselves. Although his touch was automatic, it had a curious effect on Jessica. She enjoyed being linked with Damian, enjoyed having his body close to hers. She'd experienced it while they were dancing, too.

"You ready to head back?" Damian asked as they neared the brightly lit arched entryway to Cannon Beach.

She agreed with a nod, but in fact she didn't want the night to end. Their time together had been perfect. Perhaps now Damian would understand that it was *his* company she sought and not his brother's. Perhaps now he'd view her as a woman and not the pesky girl next door.

And maybe Evan's obvious attraction to Romilda would blossom into something more, and the Drydens would stop looking to Jessica for solutions. She sincerely hoped that was the case. A man always enjoyed a challenge, and the dignitary's daughter might be just the thing Evan needed.

Damian and Jessica walked along the sawdust-covered ground of the parking lot until they reached his car. The lights from the carnival lit up the night sky, and the sounds droned on behind her.

"I had a marvelous time," she told Damian as he started the engine.

"Me, too," he said. "It's been years since I've been to Cannon Beach. Years since—" He stopped abruptly.

Jessica was reminded of what she'd heard about Damian's working too hard and not taking time to enjoy life. It felt good to know that Damian had enjoyed her company. The memory of his laughter produced a sudden smile. He didn't laugh often enough, and when he did she felt as if she'd been rewarded with a priceless gift.

Damian drove Jessica to her apartment building. It was after eleven by then, but she was keyed up with excitement. Somehow she felt it would all end when Damian left, and she wasn't ready to let that happen.

"Do you want to come up?" she asked, not really expecting he would, hoping she could change his mind.

He glanced her way as though judging the sincerity of her offer. "All right."

"I'll put on a pot of coffee, and you can gloat over how much I enjoyed the roller coaster."

"I'll gloat, coffee or not." He found a parking spot on the street, got out of the car and then went around to open her door. A true gentleman, she thought not for the first time.

Laughing and joking they strolled toward her building. The doorman held the door for them and smiled at Jessica and the purple elephant.

The laughing and teasing continued as they stepped into the elevator for the ride up to the tenth floor. The doors glided shut and Jessica sagged against the mirrored wall in mock exhaustion.

"You sure you don't want to close your eyes?" he said.

"Why?"

"This elevator is moving at death-defying speeds. Who knows the last time it was checked for safety."

"Thursday," came her glib reply.

Damian laughed delightedly.

"I don't know," she teased. "You might be right." Jokingly she squinted her eyes closed, but when she did, Damian kissed her.

It took Jessica a moment to realize what had happened. Damian had actually kissed her. It was a simple, uncomplicated kiss, the kind a brother gives a sister. One pair of lips touching another.

Only it didn't *feel* simple.

If anything, it left her longing for much, much more. Dumbstruck, she blinked up at him, not knowing how to respond.

"Don't look so shocked," Damian muttered.

"I..." She closed her mouth to stop herself from asking him to kiss her again.

"It was just a kiss."

"I know," she muttered. She realized he regretted the impulse and wished she knew of some way to tell him how thoroughly she'd enjoyed it. But before she could find the words, the elevator stopped.

Jessica led the way to her apartment and unlocked the door. Turning on the light, she moved into the cheery yellow kitchen and, as was her habit, flipped the switch to her answering machine. Cathy Hudson's voice greeted her.

"Jess. Hi, it's me. I haven't heard from you in days, and of course I want to know how the barbecue went with Lover Boy today. Give me a call when you can."

"So your friend knows about Evan?" Damian asked casually, making himself comfortable at her round oak table. He leafed through a newsmagazine she'd been reading that morning.

"I might have mentioned him, but certainly not as Lover Boy, if that's what you're asking."

"That's not what she said."

"She's teasing," Jessica insisted. She hadn't talked to her friend about her new feelings for Damian and was sorry now, because Cathy, like everyone else, it seemed, was intensely curious about the relationship between Jessica and Evan. "I made the mistake of telling her I once had a crush on Evan and she assumed... Well, you just heard." Jessica took out the coffee canister and poured some grounds into the paper filter. The rich coffee aroma filled the room. "This will only take a minute," she promised.

"Listen, don't bother. It's later than I realized."

"You're sure?" Jessica said, disappointed.

"Positive." He set aside the magazine and stood. Pausing in front of her, he drew his hand against the side of her face. "Thank you for a wonderful day, Jessica."

"Thank *you,*" she whispered back.

The apartment seemed unnaturally empty when Damian was gone. She'd hoped he'd kiss her again before he left. He'd been tempted, she could see it in his eyes, but he'd resisted, apparently wanting to keep an emotional distance from her.

Jessica wasn't at all tired and, needing to talk, dialed her friend's number.

A groggy Cathy answered on the fourth ring.

"I didn't wake you, did I?" Jessica said with a giggle, delighted to pay back her friend for all the times Cathy had phoned her in the middle of the night.

"From the dead. What are you doing calling so late and sounding so damned cheerful? There should be a law against that. Let me guess. You were with Evan."

"No! Damian and I went to the—"

"Damian? You're dating Evan's brother?" Cathy sounded wide-awake now and interested. Very interested.

"I know in that silly romantic heart of yours you figured once I was working with Evan, all the unrequited love I'd stored up years ago would suddenly blossom."

"Those were my thoughts exactly," Cathy said.

"Cathy, listen to me. Evan Dryden is a terrific guy, but he isn't the man for me."

"How can you be so sure?"

"Because...well, because I just am." Even now it was difficult to talk about her feelings for Damian. She wasn't sure how to describe them. "For one thing, Evan's in no emotional shape to get involved in another romance, which is fine by me."

"What happened?" Cathy demanded. "I thought he asked you to his family's barbecue."

"He did, but only because Damian prompted him. By the time I arrived he'd met a lovely European woman and the two were inseparable."

"How rude!"

If she'd had her heart set on Evan it would have been devastating, but she didn't, and as a consequence she'd spent a glorious night in Damian's company. She wouldn't have traded the evening for anything. "No, not at all," she said.

"You aren't disappointed?"

Apparently Cathy wasn't as awake as Jessica had believed. "Not in the least. Damian and I drove out to Cannon Beach and rode the roller coaster."

"You? The original wimp on that monster ride? You didn't really, did you?"

"Yes, I did," she announced proudly, "and it was fabulous." She spent the next few minutes relaying the highlights of the evening—Damian's winning the stuffed elephant for her and their walking along the pier and sharing cotton candy. When she finished there was a short silence.

"Hmm," said Cathy thoughtfully. "This could be *very* interesting."

JESSICA ARRIVED bright and early at the office Monday morning. Evan had apparently been to work at some point during the weekend, for he'd left her a list of instructions. His notes included a series of laws he needed her to research. Jessica got to the task right away.

Damian found her in the library some time later. "So you *are* here," he said, sounding surprised. "Mrs. Sterling didn't think you'd come in for the day. I phoned your apartment and got the answering machine."

Jessica straightened in her chair and arched her back, hoping to relieve the tension in her tired muscles. A glance at her watch told her it was nearly eleven. She'd been so involved in her research she hadn't noticed the time.

"I've been in here all morning," she explained, pinching the bridge of her nose. The words were beginning to blur in front of her eyes. Some of the reading was dull, but there were several cases she found intriguing.

Damian left and returned a moment later with a steaming cup of coffee. "Here," he said, handing it to her. "Take a break before you go blind."

"Has Evan shown up yet?" The coffee tasted like ambrosia.

Damian sighed. "Not yet. But Evan comes and goes at will, or at least he has for the past several months."

"Well, he left me some work to do, so he must have been in yesterday." She paused. "What about him and Romilda?" She sincerely hoped those two were enthralled with each other.

"It's too soon to tell, but maybe there's some hope there." Good. Damian sounded as if he really meant it.

"I want Evan to be happy," she said, not exactly sure why it was important Damian know that.

"Exactly." Damian smiled and got up to walk over to the polished bookcase. He pulled down a well-used volume. "Take some advice," he said tucking the book under his arm.

"Sure."

"Don't skip lunch."

"I won't," she promised.

He left then and Jessica smiled and closed her eyes. After a moment she returned to her research. A long time passed before her smile faded.

As promised, Jessica took her lunch hour and returned to find Evan searching for her. He sat down next to her in the library and reviewed her notes, asked a series of intelligent questions and made comments every now and then about her progress. Several times he praised her efforts. He made a few notations himself, and they spent the better part of an hour discussing different aspects of the Earl Kress case.

After Evan left, Jessica was exhilarated. Damian had revealed a keen insight into his brother's personality by assigning Evan to this important case. Representing Earl Kress had given Evan the challenge he needed; had given him a purpose, a cause. Evan was no slouch. He was dynamic, sharp and dedicated to representing this former athlete to the best of his ability and to the full extent of the law.

Several hours of research remained, and although it was late, Jessica decided to trudge on until she was finished.

"It's six o'clock and time for you to go home," Damian said from behind her in the tone she recognized. It was the one he used when he wouldn't listen to a word of argument. The kind that swayed juries.

"I'll be finished in a bit."

"You're finished now."

"Damian."

"Don't argue with me, Jessica. It won't do any good."

She closed the book she was reading and stood up. Every small movement of her lithe body spelled reluctance.

"Did you take time for lunch?"

"You're beginning to sound like my guardian!"

"I see you didn't eat, otherwise you wouldn't be snapping at me."

"I did so—and I'm not snapping!"

"That does it!"

Was he about to fire her for insubordination? Jessica wondered. She stared up at him, wondering what would happen next.

"We're going to dinner," he muttered.

"Dinner! But Damian, you've already—"

"Pizza," he said, "the deep-dish variety. There's a small Italian restaurant around the corner. I swear it's one of the best-kept secrets in Boston."

"Pizza," Jessica repeated slowly and her stomach growled in anticipation. "Well, if you insist, and it seems that you do." She reached for her purse.

They walked to the restaurant, which was nestled in the basement of one of the older buildings. The marble floors were badly worn, and the architecture showed that the structure had been built in the early thirties. Jessica had passed the building a hundred times and barely given it a second's notice.

"How'd you hear about this restaurant?" she asked.

"From the security guard. He eats here regularly and recommended it to me. I've never tasted better Italian food."

The proprietor greeted Damian as if he were a long-lost cousin, kissing him on both cheeks and speaking in Italian as he looked approvingly at Jessica.

"What did he say?" she asked when they were seated at a table covered with a red-and-white-checked cloth. A candle flickered from inside a small red vase, and shadows danced across the opposite wall.

"I'm not entirely sure. I only know a few words myself."

"In that case you did a good job of faking it."

"All right, if you must know, Antonio assumed we're lovers," Damian said casually, opening the menu.

"You corrected him, didn't you?" she demanded, putting a hand to her chest. She could feel the color rush into her face.

"No."

"Damian, you can't let that man believe you and I..."

"You're probably right, I shouldn't. Especially when it's my brother you're in love with, not me."

Jessica set the menu aside and leaned forward until her stomach pressed against the edge of the table. They needed to get this straight between them once and for all. "I'm not in love with Evan," she whispered heatedly.

"All right, all right."

"You don't sound convinced."

"I'm convinced," he said, without looking at her. Whatever was offered on the menu had apparently captured his full attention.

"Good," she said, reaching for her own menu. She was about to suggest the sausage pizza when a basket of warm bread was brought to their table. The lovely dark-haired woman who'd delivered it caught Damian's face between her hands and kissed him soundly on both cheeks. Jessica must have looked shocked, because the older woman laughed delightedly. "You don't need to worry—I won't steal Damian away from you," she said, then added something in Italian.

Damian seemed to go pale at the woman's words. Jessica's own knowledge of Italian was scant, but she knew what *bambino* meant.

"Damian, tell me what she said."

He was silent while the same woman poured them each a glass of wine and brought a plate of antipasto. Then he sighed. "Nona says you seem good and sturdy."

"*What?* Anyway, she said more than that."

"Jessica, I already explained I only know a few words of Italian."

"You know more than me. She said *bambino*. Doesn't that mean 'baby'?"

Damian sighed again. "Yes. If you must know, Nona said you'll make a good mother to my children."

"Oh." Jessica glanced at the woman, who was standing on the other side of the room, busy ladling minestrone soup into two ceramic bowls, which she then brought.

"I guess we aren't going to get that pizza," Damian muttered after the soup was served.

Antonio returned with the bottle of Italian wine and replenished their glasses with many exclamations of pleasure. Damian thanked him in Italian, then they spoke for a minute or two.

"When did you learn to speak Italian?" Jessica asked.

"I didn't. I picked up a smidgen here and there over the years. I spent a couple of months in Italy before I entered law school and muddled my way through the country. That's about it."

"You're a man of many talents," she said, picking up her spoon and sampling the soup. It was rich and flavorful. In fact, everything was excellent—the meal, the smooth red wine, the cappucino and dessert. Each time she was convinced she couldn't swallow another bite, Nona would bring them something else she insisted they try.

"Either we leave now, or you'll have to roll me out of here," Jessica said.

Damian chuckled, settled the bill, and together they walked back to the office high rise. The evening was glorious, and Jessica felt wonderful. She wasn't sure if it was the result of the weather, the delicious food and wine or the company—or maybe all of them.

"Thank you," she said in the elevator.

"You're welcome." Damian fell strangely quiet as they walked to the law library. Before she left for the night, Jessica wanted to shelve the volumes she'd been studying. Damian worked silently with her. When they were finished, he preceded her from the room, automatically turning off the light.

The room was suddenly dark and Jessica bumped into a table.

"Jessica."

"I'm fine," she assured him, walking toward the hall light.

"That's the problem," he muttered, reaching for her. She was in his arms before she realized it. "I'm not." With that his mouth came down on hers.

CHAPTER FIVE

THIS KISS WASN'T brotherly, nor was it uncomplicated. Damian's mouth fit over hers, warm and coaxing. Jessica sighed and relaxed against him, giving herself up to the sensation. It felt *right* to be in his arms, that was all there was to it.

Her hands gripped the lapels of his jacket, her fingers crushing the soft wool as his mouth moved against hers. Damian's hand curved around the side of her neck, his touch tender as though he feared hurting her.

The kiss was unlike any Jessica had ever experienced. She felt the sensual power of it all the way to her toes, the impact stealing her breath. She moaned and Damian did, too. When they broke apart, neither spoke. Jessica wished he'd say something, anything, to break the silence. She needed him to explain what was happening, because she was lost, taken by surprise, yet delighted to the very depths of her being.

Instead, Damian turned and walked away.

She couldn't believe it. A tear slipped unnoticed down her cheek and dropped onto her silk blouse, the droplet bleeding into a small circle. She raised her hand to her face, surprised by the tear.

Funny that when she couldn't find the words to say what she felt, a tear would speak for her. She'd learned that lesson years earlier. Her mother's tears had fallen onto her grandmother's casket, and they had said far more than a whispered farewell. Tearstains on a letter revealed more than its words.

A tear on her cheek now, after she'd shared a kiss with this man, spelled out volumes. Only to Jessica the language was one she couldn't fully understand.

The sudden need to escape overwhelmed her. Collecting her purse, she stepped out of the library and proceeded down the hallway. She paused outside Damian's open door. She saw him standing in front of his window, looking into the night. His hands were clasped behind his back.

"Good night," she called softly.

He turned and smiled briefly. "Good night, Jessica. See you in the morning."

She wished they could sit down and discuss what had happened, but one look told her Damian was confused and not nearly as delighted as she was. He seemed troubled, burdened somehow. She wondered if he regretted having kissed her.

"Thank you for dinner," she said. "You were right. It's the best Italian food I've ever had." She didn't want to leave, but didn't have an excuse to stay.

"I'm glad you enjoyed it."

Jessica headed for the elevator. Her thoughts remained so muddled that she nearly missed her subway stop on the ride home. The first thing she did when she walked into her apartment was reach for the purple elephant Damian had won for her. She wrapped her arms around it and hugged it tight. It made her feel close to Damian. All she needed to do was shut her eyes and the memories of their night together at Cannon Beach filled her mind. She could almost hear the sound of the carousel, the echo of her own laughter when Damian insisted on winning her the elephant. She could hear the roller coaster as the riders shrieked past and smell the popcorn, candy apples and hot dogs.

Keeping the elephant pressed to her, Jessica slumped into the overstuffed chair and reached for her phone, dialing the number of her best friend. Cathy was far more insightful in these matters than she was. She would help her make sense of Damian's kiss.

"Hi," Jessica murmured when her friend answered.

Her greeting was met with a slight hesitation. "What's wrong?"

It didn't surprise her that her friend knew her so well. "What makes you think anything's wrong?"

"I recognize that tone of voice."

Smiling to herself, Jessica brought up her knees and rested her chin there as she assembled her thoughts. There didn't seem to be an easy way of explaining what had happened. Best just to blurt it out. "Damian kissed me tonight."

"And you liked it, didn't you?"

Cathy sounded gleeful, as though tempted to break into song. Jessica supposed this was what she got for having a theater-arts major for a best friend.

"Yeah—but I'm totally confused," Jessica admitted quietly. This jumble of mixed feelings was the main source of her troubles.

"Surprises you, doesn't it?" Cathy asked, then chuckled softly, again with that note of delight. "I've seen the handwriting on the wall ever since you mentioned Damian Saturday night. The guy sounds perfect for you."

"Don't be ridiculous. "

"What's ridiculous about it?"

"I haven't thought of him . . . that way. Well, I have recently, and frankly, it frightens me to death. I've already made a fool of myself over one Dryden. I'm not anxious to make the same mistake with another one."

"You were a kid the first time. There's a world of difference between what happened then and what's happening now."

"Maybe," was all Jessica was willing to concede.

"Think, woman," Cathy said dramatically. "The man's obviously attracted to you, too. Otherwise he wouldn't be kissing you."

"I don't know that, and you don't, either. We kissed, and then he acted as if it was the worst thing he could have done. He didn't say a word and he just walked away. I don't know what to think. I'm so confused." She pressed a hand to her forehead.

"So you think he regretted it?"

"He must have. Otherwise . . . otherwise everything would have turned out differently. He looked at me as if I were a stranger, as if he didn't want to see me again."

"What was he supposed to do? Confess undying love? Didn't you tell me you had the whole situation figured out? The only reason Damian hired you in the first place was to bolster his brother's spirits. Think about it, Jess—the man has integrity. He can't very well start dating you himself if he believes you might still have some feeling for his younger brother."

"It drives me crazy that he'd think that!"

"I know, but you've got to look at it from his point of view."

"At the cost of my own sanity?"

"For now," Cathy said sympathetically.

"I don't know what to do!" Jessica cried, amazed at the amount of emotion that spilled into the words.

"There's more," Cathy said, warming to the subject. "If you're interested in Damian, it makes perfect sense that you're going to have to be the one to make the first move. Damian's hands are tied as long as he thinks there's the least chance you're interested in his brother. The guy's in a real bind here."

"Him! This whole thing with Evan's gotten out of hand. The poor guy's suffocating with everyone's concern. I actually feel sorry for him. He got the raw end of a deal in a relationship, and all he needed was some time to work out his pain," Jessica lamented. "Instead, Damian cut his work load until he's bored out of his mind. His parents, especially his mother, are dishing out sympathy by the truckload, and it's all Evan can do to stay afloat."

She paused for breath, then went on, "The only reason Damian hired me was that he thought I'd pull Evan out of the doldrums. I haven't talked to Evan, but I'm sure he resents all this nonsense. And I don't blame him."

"What about you and Damian?"

"I don't know what to think," Jessica admitted. "I wish I did. If he's interested in me, then surely it's his place to say or do something. Regardless of how he thinks I feel about Evan."

"Oh, come on, Jess!"

"I know Damian."

"Huh. You thought you knew Evan, too."

"I do, or rather, I did," she argued. The conversation was frustrating her more by the minute. "Besides, like I said earlier, I'm not interested in making a fool of myself over another Dryden. I learned my lesson the last time. Good grief, that was years ago and my parents and his *still* talk about it. Just this last weekend my own mother mentioned how pleased she'd be if I married Evan!"

"I have an idea," Cathy said slowly as though the scheme was taking shape in her mind as she spoke. "Introduce me to Damian."

"What possible reason do you have to meet him?" Jessica didn't like the sound of this.

"I just want to. Things aren't going well with David...."

"David?" Jessica cried. "Who's David?"

"The director for *Guys and Dolls*. Now listen, I know this sounds crazy, but trust me, it could work."

"What could work?" Jessica was fast losing what remained of her patience.

"Our meeting. I'll turn on the charm, do what I can to enchant him, and—"

"Just a minute, Cath, you're talking about the man *I'm* interested in."

"I know," she replied as if all this was perfectly logical. "But you want to know how serious he is about you, don't you? Also, maybe watching him with another woman will help you sort out *your* feelings for *him*.

"Yes, but—"

"Come on, Jess. You said yourself you weren't willing to make a fool of yourself a second time. This way you'll know."

"This sounds silly to me."

"Not only that," Cathy went on as though Jessica hadn't spoken, "it'll give me a chance to practice some of my best lines. Just introduce us, and I promise I won't do anything to embarrass you."

"All right," she agreed without any real enthusiasm. "How do you propose we do this?"

"I could stop by the office one day soon and suggest lunch. It'd be natural for you to introduce me around, wouldn't it?"

"I...suppose, but doesn't that seem a bit obvious?"

"Perhaps. Do you have a better idea?"

"No." She sighed. "Okay. Do you want me to invite Damian to join us? I'm coming into the office this Saturday to catch up on a few things, before Evan's big court case starts next week. My guess is that Damian will be there, as well."

"All the better, then. I'll see you Saturday around noon."

Jessica hedged. "You're sure about this?"

"Absolutely! I have ways of getting a man to talk."

"That sounds like something out of a movie."

Cathy laughed. "It is."

"That's what I thought," she mumbled.

PRECISELY AT NOON Cathy arrived at the office. Jessica envied her petite friend her pixie good looks, short dark hair and big blue eyes. Cathy looked striking in her pants, which were black with huge white dots, and multicolored striped suspenders. Her blouse was white with small black dots and she was wearing black high heels. One thing was certain—no one would miss seeing her walk down the street. If Evan had been in the office, he doubtless would have begged an introduction.

"You must have forgotten about our lunch," Cathy said more loudly than necessary, standing outside Jessica's office. Loudly enough for Damian to hear.

Her friend's ploy worked because a minute later he wandered out of his office.

"Damian, this is my friend Cathy Hudson," Jessica said. "I might have mentioned her in passing."

Damian and Cathy shook hands. "Jessica forgot we were supposed to meet for lunch today." Cathy said.

"It isn't a good idea for Jessica to skip meals," Damian said. His eyes twinkled and the effort to suppress a smile caused the corners of his mouth to quiver.

"So you've seen what happens when Jessica's stomach growls. Wounded bears are easier to reason with than Jess when she's hungry."

"Hey, that's not true!" Jessica flared. They were speaking as if she wasn't there. She braced her hands on her hips and glared at the two of them. She hadn't been keen on this idea of Cathy's from the first and her instincts were proving to be right.

Her former roommate eased closer to Damian and was gazing soulfully into his eyes. He didn't seem to mind in the least; in fact, he seemed to lap it up.

"I'll get my purse," Jessica said stiffly, leaving Cathy and Damian gazing at each other while she went behind her desk and dug in the bottom drawer. The whole charade irritated her, and she was furious she'd allowed herself to be talked into it.

Cathy managed to tear her eyes away from Damian long enough to throw visual spikes at her friend. It took Jessica a moment to realize what was being signaled. Oh, yes—she was supposed to invite him to tag along.

"Would you care to join us for lunch?" she asked Damian, managing to sound polite, if unenthusiastic.

"Please, do," Cathy said, her words like warm honey.

Damian looked at Jessica as if seeking her confirmation, and to her credit, she did produce a smile. She didn't know why she'd ever agreed to this.

"I'll be happy to join you," Damian surprised her by saying. She'd never dreamed he would. The man was *full* of surprises.

"Great, just great," Jessica muttered under her breath.

"Fabulous," came Cathy's melodious response.

Jessica rolled her eyes, and together the three of them headed out of the office. Damian suggested a well-known expensive restaurant, and before Jessica could comment one way or another, Cathy had agreed. Jessica snapped her mouth closed before she said something she'd regret. It irked her that Damian would so easily fall into Cathy's snare. It might be just a charade, but she was left more than a little confused.

Outside the building, Damian waved down a cab, and Cathy managed to have Damian in the back seat with her. Jessica sat in the front while her best friend giggled her way through the streets of Boston. They drove past the Boston Common and the Freedom Trail, the winding yellow path that led history buffs and tourists from one historic monument to another.

She was acting like a jealous fool, Jessica realized with a start. Jealous of Damian and Cathy? The fog that had clouded her thinking for the past several days cleared.

She was falling in love with Damian Dryden. It couldn't have been any more obvious. It was one of the things Cathy had set out to prove, and her friend was right—she'd needed this blunt lesson.

Of course she loved Damian. From the minute she'd walked into his office and asked about the job. From the minute he'd stood on the footbridge that forged the pond on his parents' property and insisted on taking her to Cannon Beach.

From the minute he'd kissed her.

This was what Cathy had been trying to tell her.

When they arrived at the restaurant, Cathy excused herself and Jessica. With her arm wrapped around her friend's, she dragged her to the ladies' room.

Before Jessica could open her mouth, Cathy burst out, "Damian's wonderful!"

"I know."

"I haven't met Evan, but I'm telling you right now if you're not interested in his big brother, I am. He's got a great wit, he's gorgeous, and—"

"I know all that." And a lot more.

"Listen," Cathy said, "I want you to make some excuse and leave."

Jessica was stunned. "You want me to *what?*"

Cathy was refreshing her makeup in front of the mirror, her eyeliner in hand. "You heard me. Remember an urgent appointment, something that will call you away so the two of us can be alone together. Only don't make it sound phony, or Damian will know what we're doing.''

''*I* don't know what we're doing,'' she protested.

''I want you to give me some time alone with him.''

''Why?'' Jessica demanded. ''Listen, you've already proved your point. I do care about Damian. And I'm not interested in sharing him with you.''

''I know how you feel about him,'' Cathy said slowly as if that much had been understood from the beginning. ''But my being alone with him will tell us both how he feels about *you,* which was the main purpose of my plan.''

''You're sure about this?''

''How many times are you going to ask me? Of course I'm sure.''

''I can't help thinking we're both good candidates for psychoanalysis!''

Cathy laughed outright at that. ''Don't worry, I'm not going to steal him away from you, although heaven knows I'm tempted. The guy's a hunk. Why hasn't he ever married?''

''How am I supposed to know?''

''Have you tried asking?''

Cathy had a way of making everything sound perfectly straightforward. ''Don't worry about it. I'll find that out, along with everything else.''

Jessica hesitated. She trusted Cathy—most of the time. She also knew it wasn't beneath her best friend to say or do something sneaky. That was what worried Jessica.

"Go back to your apartment," Cathy instructed, before outlining her lush full mouth with a glossy shade of lipstick.

"I still don't understand what you're doing."

Cathy patiently closed the tube and shook her head as though to suggest the answer was obvious. "You don't need to. When Damian and I've finished lunch I can report my findings to you. Is everything clear now?"

"As mud."

Cathy rolled her eyes. "I'm trying to be a help here. The least you can do is cooperate."

"All right, all right," Jessica muttered, but she didn't like it.

"Let's not keep Prince Charming waiting any longer," Cathy said, taking Jessica's elbow. "Just remember to come up with something brilliant to excuse yourself."

Jessica was feeling anything but brilliant at the moment. "All right," she promised.

Jessica did manage to come up with a plausible excuse. They were seated and given elaborate menus decorated with gold tassels. Jessica set her purse on the floor, and it promptly fell over. When she leaned down to right it, she pulled a small appointment card from the outside pocket. Straightening, she studied the card.

"What's the date today?"

"The twelfth. Why?" Cathy's eyes had never been rounder, or more guileless.

"It says here I've got a dentist's appointment this afternoon." She made a show of looking at her watch. "In half an hour."

"On a Saturday?" Damian asked casually.

"Lots of dentists are keeping Saturday hours," Cathy explained conversationally, spreading the linen napkin across her lap. "I went in for a checkup myself no more than a month ago, and my appointment was on a Saturday."

"It's too late to call and cancel," Jessica said with a defeated air. "It took me months to get this appointment as it was. The Saturday schedule fills up quickly."

"If you made it months ago, it isn't any wonder you forgot." Cathy seemed all too willing to offer Jessica an excuse.

"I'd better see if I can catch a cab," Jessica mumbled. She wouldn't be able to keep up this charade much longer. It'd be a miracle if Damian didn't see through their plot. It had more holes than a golf course.

"I'm so sorry you have to go," Cathy said with enough sincerity to sound believable.

Damian said nothing. If Cathy's theory was true, Damian would reveal some regret at her leaving. Instead, he smiled at her and nodded as if he welcomed the time alone with her friend. Jessica's hands closed tightly around her purse strap as she stood and made her farewells.

Once she was outside, the doorman's whistle hailed her a cab. Jessica climbed into the back seat and gave the man the address of her apartment, thinking this was going to be the longest afternoon of her life.

She was right.

She paced her living room munching on pretzels for a good two hours. Most of the large bag had disappeared before her doorbell chimed. Cathy. In her eagerness to hear what she'd achieved, Jessica nearly jerked the door off its hinges.

Nothing could have surprised her more than to find Damian standing on the other side. She must have looked as dumbstruck as she felt, because he grinned and let himself in without waiting for an invitation.

"How was the dentist's appointment?"

"Ah . . . I didn't have one."

"I know." He walked over to her bookcase and was examining the titles as if he'd come for that purpose alone.

"You knew?"

"You're not nearly as good an actress as your friend," he said, turning to face her. Jessica tried to read his expression, but found it impossible. She felt rooted to the carpet, unable to move and hardly able to breathe. She wondered if he was angry with her. Perhaps he was amused. She couldn't tell which.

She should have known he'd see through their ploy. "It was a stupid plan," she admitted. Her shoulders sagged with a burden of regrets. She'd allowed Cathy to talk her into this crazy scheme, and she'd followed like a lamb to the slaughter.

"I . . . we didn't offend you, did we?"

A hint of a smile touched his eyes. "No, it was a very sweet thing to do, but unnecessary."

She blinked, not knowing what to say because she wasn't sure she understood.

Damian walked over to her and reached out a hand to press against her cheek. His touch was gentle, his gray eyes as serious as she'd ever seen them. He spoke as though his words pained him. "I appreciate your efforts, Jessica, but I can find my own dates." Then he bent and gently placed his mouth on hers. The kiss was far too short to satisfy her. Instead, it created a need for more. When he lifted his head, everything within her wanted to beg him not to stop.

"I'll see you Monday morning," he said, turning and heading toward the door.

She opened her mouth to tell him to stay, but by the time she could get the words out he was gone. He actually believed she was setting him up with Cathy. No wonder. That was exactly what it looked like. Why hadn't she thought of this before? Jessica slumped onto her sofa, covered her face with her hands and resisted the urge to cry.

Damian hadn't been gone for more than five minutes when Cathy arrived. Jessica opened her door to find her friend leaning against the doorjamb as if she needed its support. She threw herself down on Jessica's couch and removed her high heels. "That man's a tough nut to crack."

Jessica folded her arms and asked, "What do you mean?"

"I mean he was so closemouthed about you, there's only one sensible conclusion."

"And what's that?"

Cathy stopped rubbing her toes and turned her big blue eyes on Jessica. "You're serious? You mean you really don't know?"

"I wouldn't be asking if I did!"

"He's in love with you."

Jessica didn't believe it. "He can't be."

"Why can't he? Is there a law posted somewhere that says it's a crime to fall in love with Jessica Kellerman?"

"No..."

"He wasn't interested in me, and trust me, I tried."

Jessica stiffened, remembering her reaction to Cathy's attempts to flirt with Damian. She hadn't liked it. None of the crazy stunts her friend had pulled over the years had put their friendship on the line. This one had. Damian was off-limits, and before Cathy left for home, Jessica wanted to make sure she knew it.

"He thought I was trying to set him up with you," Jessica muttered disparagingly.

"What's so tragic about that? That was exactly what I wanted him to think."

"But why?"

Cathy's smile was slow and confident. "This is the reason I'm your best friend. My little performance this afternoon was for both your benefits. You know how you feel about Damian, too. I'm right, aren't I?"

Jessica nodded reluctantly, hating to admit her friend's ploy had worked. But there was a problem. "Damian assumes I was setting him up with you because I'm not interested in him."

"What makes you think that?"

"'Think' nothing. He practically said so."

"When?"

"Just a few minutes ago. He was here. The whole experiment backfired, Cath."

"You straightened him out, didn't you?"

"No... I didn't get the chance." Jessica felt worse and worse. She had no one to blame but herself. She'd allowed Cathy to talk her into this crazy scheme, and now she was suffering the consequences.

Cathy went uncharacteristically quiet. "You'll talk to him, won't you?"

"I . . . I don't know. I suppose so."

"Good. Explain how you feel, otherwise he'll go right on thinking you're not interested."

Jessica closed here eyes and groaned.

"It won't be hard," Cathy assured her. "He's crazy about you, Jess."

When her former roommate left a few minutes later, Jessica realized what a good friend Cathy had always been—despite her penchant for theatrics.

JESSICA CONSIDERED Cathy's advice for what remained of the weekend and arrived at the office early Monday morning. To her surprise, Evan was sitting at his desk when she walked in. He smiled broadly in greeting. "Good morning, sweet Jessica." He seemed to be in an awfully good mood. His brown eyes were clear and lively, and his smile was warm. "You're just the person I was waiting to see."

She stowed her purse and moved into his office with a pen and pad, fully expecting him to give her another lengthy assignment.

"Sit down," he instructed, motioning her toward a chair on the other side of his desk. He leaned back in his own chair, looking relaxed. "Now tell me something."

"Sure." Her mind was churning with a possible list of requests.

"I've been something of a bad boy around here lately, not pulling my own weight and the like. You know that, don't you?"

"I . . . I've only been in the office a short time," she said, not wanting to speak out of turn. "It's not for me to say if you have or haven't been doing your share of the work."

"Really, Jess, there's no need to be shy."

"All right," she said, resenting the fact that she'd been put in this position. "I know you were hurt, but we all face disappointments in life. It's time to pull yourself up by your bootstraps."

Evan laughed delightedly, not the least bit offended. "By heaven, I like a woman who can speak her mind."

Jessica relaxed and uncrossed her legs. "Was that all?"

"No." He tipped back in his chair and rubbed the side of his face while studying her carefully. "There was a time when you were rather...keen on me, wasn't there?"

"Yes." She flushed. "Years ago."

"You worshiped me from afar, so to speak."

She lowered her gaze and nodded.

"You're right about my being disappointed," he went on. "I felt the need to prove myself. In looking back, I realize how shallow I've been. I'm not proud of my behavior these past few months, and I'm hoping to make up for it with the Earl Kress trial."

Jessica didn't know how to comment or even if she should.

"My father and I had a good long talk this weekend," Evan added thoughtfully.

"I understand he's considering running for the Senate."

"Yes, and he's decided to give it a shot. Damian and I will be spending a fair amount of time working on his campaign. The gist of our conversation was simple. He wants me to get my life straightened out and start dating again."

"I think he's absolutely right," she agreed readily, assuming Evan was referring to the diplomat's daughter.

"Great." He beamed her a killer smile. "I was hoping you'd feel that way."

Jessica blinked, not grasping what he meant. "Why's that?"

"Because, my dear Jessie, I've decided I'd like to get to know you better. You're very sweet and a hell of a good worker. Dad reminded me that you were keen on me a few years back, and I'm hoping to capitalize on your affection."

"Ah..." Now didn't seem the appropriate moment to bring up her feelings for Damian. Then again, she'd better before matters got out of hand.

"I don't mind telling you," Evan said before she could speak, "my confidence has been badly shaken. I feel safe and secure with you. Frankly, I don't know how I'd deal with any more rejection."

CHAPTER SIX

"AREN'T YOU SEEING Romilda?" Jessica asked with a sinking feeling. She *had* to say something, set the record straight, but Evan was studying her with an eager intensity, and coward that she was, Jessica couldn't make herself do it. "You seemed to get along so well with her at the barbecue, and her political connections might help your father's campaign efforts."

"She's already returned to Europe."

"I see."

"Don't get me wrong, Romilda's a sweetheart, but she isn't the one for me," Evan explained. "I want an old-fashioned girl, who values the same things I do. Mom, home, apple pie—that sort of thing. A woman who knows what's really important in life. Someone like you, Jessica."

Jessica didn't doubt for an instant that Evan was echoing his father's words. Maybe the sort of woman he described *was* right for him, but Jessica wasn't the one. She was about to explain diplomatically that there was already someone in her life—without telling him who—when he spoke again.

"I've got a ton of work waiting for me this morning, but my parents asked that we meet later, and I thought the five of us could have lunch together."

"Five?"

"Damian will be there, too. Would noon be convenient?"

"Ah . . ."

"Great." He returned his attention to the papers on his desk. Jessica waited a moment, then got up and went back to the outer office. She felt the blood drain out of her face as she reached her desk and sat down.

"Is Mr. Dryden here?" Jessica hadn't been aware of Mrs. Sterling's arrival.

Jessica looked up and nodded.

"But it's barely nine."

"I know," she murmured.

"What's come over that man?" the secretary murmured, unable to disguise her amazement. "Never mind, let's not question it. I'd rather count my blessings. I was about to lose heart with him. I was afraid Damian had given Evan too much slack the past few months."

Jessica managed a weak smile. Mrs. Sterling moved about the office with the efficiency that was her trademark. She brewed a pot of coffee and the aroma of the rich Colombian helped revive Jessica. When the coffee was ready, Mrs. Sterling poured Evan a cup and carried it into his office. Jessica couldn't hear what was being said, but apparently Evan was in top form, because his secretary returned grinning broadly.

Jessica sat at her desk, too numb to think clearly. She'd missed her golden opportunity, if indeed there'd been one, to tell Evan she was in love with Damian. Yet it didn't seem fair to make such a confession to his brother when she hadn't said a word to Damian. Nor was she convinced Damian felt the same way about her. All she had to go on was Cathy's faith.

Her theatrical friend had a tendency to exaggerate, to expand the truth and fill it with an enthusiasm that simply might not exist. Damian was fond of her, Jessica didn't doubt that, but as for his being in love with her, Jessica couldn't say.

There was nothing to do but sit by patiently and wait to see how matters developed. Evan was making this effort for his father; it didn't mean he intended their relationship to be anything but show. Certainly he wasn't serious about wooing her. Not when he'd cared so deeply for this unknown Mary Jo.

The morning passed quickly as they prepared for the Earl Kress trial, slated to begin the following day. The attention generated by the local television stations was sure to spark interest in the law firm and in Evan's father's bid for the Senate. In addition, the trial had the potential to affect the outcome of education in school districts across the country.

Close to noon, Evan emerged from his office, and with a warm smile at Jessica, said to his secretary, "I'm going to steal this lovely one away from you for a couple of hours."

Mrs. Sterling nodded approvingly.

Jessica reached for her purse and stood, hoping this lunch would afford her a few minutes alone with Damian so they could talk. She desperately needed to discuss things with him, to explain what had happened and seek his counsel.

To Jessica's disappointment, the opportunity never arose. The three met Evan's parents at the Hilton. The meal was pleasant and cordial, and everyone seemed to be in a good mood—with the exception of Damian, who practically ignored Jessica. She might have been invisible for all the attention he paid her.

She decided to make an effort to let her feelings for the older Dryden son be known, and she waited until there was a lull in the conversation.

"Damian and I were out to Cannon Beach recently," she announced brightly after their salads were served. Evan's parents exchanged meaningful glances.

"From here on out Evan will be the one taking you to the beach, isn't that right?" Damian said to his brother.

"You should have said something earlier, Jess," Evan said, picking up on Damian's cue. "I love Cannon Beach. We'll make a point of going there sometime, all right? As soon as the Earl Kress trial's over."

"All right," Jessica agreed, her heart in her throat. She looked to Damian, who was busy eating his salad. From all outward appearances, it made no difference to him whom she dated. Apparently the idea of Evan's holding her close while they rode on the roller coaster didn't trouble him. Not at all.

After lunch they made their way into one of the meeting rooms on the second level of the hotel, where a news conference was scheduled. There, Walter Dryden, surrounded by his wife and family, announced his intention to run for the Senate.

Mingling in the audience of newsmen, well-wishers and political-party members, Jessica was able to stand back and view the four Drydens. They were a handsome, wholesome family who believed in the American dream. She admired and loved them, and wished Walter Dryden every success.

Flashbulbs exploded around her as she wandered to the back of the room. She wasn't sure why Evan had insisted she attend this affair, other than to reassure his father he'd taken their father-son talk to heart.

Jessica knew that life was often filled with ironic twists such as this, but why did hers have to be so frustrating? She was pretty sure Evan's father had put the idea of dating her into his son's head. And why not? It was well-known she'd once had a crush on Evan. And their families were so close. She was the logical choice, and the fact that she now worked for Evan made it all the more convenient.

The younger Dryden hoped to enhance his image, assist his father in his campaign efforts and prove he was over a painful relationship. What better way to start than with a woman who'd once had stars in her eyes for him?

Except that those stars were focused in another direction now. On his older brother. A man who seemed determined to do the noble thing and step aside for his brother.

For the first time in months, Evan had revealed a willingness to put the past behind him and get on with his life. And Damian believed she was the reason he had. So he would do nothing to change that—even if he did love her himself.

EVERY DAY for the next week the Dryden name turned up in all the media. The television and radio stations followed the trial, and each afternoon the newspaper carried an account of what had happened in the courtroom. Jessica met Earl Kress the first time in the courtroom and was impressed with the young man's sincerity. He wasn't looking to cripple the school system with a huge monetary settlement; instead, he sought changes that would help other athletes. Evan had arranged for a private tutor for the young man. Earl hoped to return to college within a year and work toward a degree in education. His goal was to teach high school students himself.

The more she learned about Evan's generosity to Earl, the more impressed she was with the lawyer's generous heart. Earl had been cheated out of his education, and Evan had made it his mission to make sure this didn't happen to future generations.

At the same time, Walter Dryden was making a splash across the various media. It seemed there was a social engagement every night of the week having to do with the upcoming primary. Because of his involvement with the trial, Evan wasn't expected to attend these functions. For that Jessica was grateful, although she knew Damian had become actively involved in his father's campaign. She yearned to talk to him, but he seemed to be avoiding her. She rarely saw him, and when she did he was occupied with someone else.

On Friday the jury convened. Jessica returned to the office, preferring not to wait at the courthouse for the outcome of the trial. Evan had built a strong case and she was confident Earl would win his suit, but waiting for the jury's verdict was agony.

The office buzzed with activity, the way it generally did in the afternoons. There was the hum of computers, fax machines and photocopiers, and messengers zigzagged from one room to the next, crowding the hallways. The whole place was filled with an air of expectancy.

Jessica walked over to her desk, removed her shoes and rubbed her sore toes against her calves. Her muscles ached, and she was mentally and emotionally exhausted. This had been an incredibly hectic week. As soon as she got home, she was going to soak in a hot tub and curl up with a good book. Sleeping until noon the next day held irresistible appeal.

Mrs. Sterling had left on an errand and Jessica had just slumped down in her chair when Damian strolled into the office. He stopped abruptly when he saw she was alone.

Jessica froze, her breath trapped in her lungs.

"Hello, Jessica," he said stiffly.

"Hello," she managed.

"Where's Mrs. Sterling?" he asked, recovering first. He was brisk and businesslike, as if he'd never held her in his arms, as if she'd never been more to him than a friend, a casual one at that.

"Off on an errand," she answered, then added, "The jury's still out."

"So I understand." He walked over to Mrs. Sterling's desk and set a stack of papers in the secretary's in-basket.

"Have you been to that Italian restaurant lately?" she asked, desperate to make conversation. Desperate to remind him of the good times they'd shared—and what had happened afterward. She yearned with all her being that he understood her message—that those times had meant the world to her and that she hoped they'd been important to him, too. She prayed he'd realize how much she missed him.

"I haven't dined out lately." Then he turned abruptly and strode from the room.

Hurt and angry, Jessica wanted to shout at him to come back. But it wouldn't have done any good; she knew that. He'd sliced her out of his life without a second thought, and apparently without a single regret.

About an hour later, Evan burst into the office. He paused just inside the doorway, threw back his head and released a yell loud enough to sway the light fixtures.

"We did it!"

Startled, Jessica looked up from her desk. She stood to offer him her congratulations, and Evan rushed to her, lifting her high off the ground and whirling her around. "We won!" he shouted.

"Evan!" She laughed, bracing her hands on his shoulders. He was spinning so fast she was growing dizzy.

His cries of jubilation had attracted the attention of others in the office, but Evan didn't show any signs of releasing her. He set her back down on the ground and, looping his arm around her shoulders, kept her close to his side. Words of congratulations were enthusiastically offered.

"I couldn't have done it without Jessica," he announced to the gathering. "Her research was invaluable. Damian, too," Evan said, holding his free arm out to his brother. "A man couldn't ask for a better brother."

Jessica was looking at Damian, and whether he'd intended it or not—she suspected he hadn't—their eyes met. His guard had lowered, and his expression was one of such emotional intensity that nothing could have pulled her gaze from his. In him she read pride, loyalty and devotion. In him she saw that there was nothing on this earth he would do or say to hurt his brother, even at the sacrifice of his own happiness.

Tears clouded her vision. Gazing into the faces of those around her, she forced herself to smile, forced herself to look as though this was the happiest moment of her life, when on the inside, she'd never felt more miserable.

Evan insisted on taking her to dinner that night to celebrate. A victory gala, he told her. He chose a restaurant well known for its superb food and service, and Jessica knew when they were seated that she was the envy of every woman there. Evan had never looked more handsome or been more charming.

They were leaving the restaurant, waiting for the valet to bring around Evan's car, when a news photographer stopped them and took their picture. Jessica protested, but Evan told her that this was the price of fame and she might as well smile.

The next morning, Jessica's mother phoned before she'd had a chance to awake, and hours before she'd intended to. She was extremely depressed, and sleep was the perfect escape.

"Jessica, have you seen it?" Joyce demanded, her voice raised with excitement. "I've already called the newspaper and am having them make copies for Lois and me. You both look fabulous."

"Seen what, Mother?" was the groggy reply.

"The newspaper, sweetheart. There's a picture of you and Evan on the society page with a nice little write-up. In case you didn't see it, your name was mentioned in the gossip column, too, on Thursday, linking you with Evan. Oh, honey, I'm so pleased."

"Oh, Lord," Jessica whispered, her mind clouded with exhaustion. "I remember now. A photographer stopped us last night."

"Yes, I know, that's what I've been telling you. The picture's in this morning's paper. I'm thrilled and so is your father, not to mention Lois and Walter."

Jessica was anything but thrilled. "It's only a picture, Mom."

"It's more than that, Jessica. It's a dream come true for you, and for me, too. You've always felt so strongly about Evan and now, after all these years, he feels the same way about you."

"Mother, you don't understand, Evan and I—"

"You don't know how pleased Lois and I are. We realize it's much too soon to be making wedding plans, but it's the sort of thing good friends love to do when their children are dating. You're our only daughter, and I can tell you right now this will be the gala event of the year. Your father and I insist."

She only paused long enough to take a breath, then rushed on, "We'd be so very pleased if you and Evan decided to have an autumn wedding. Lois has been my friend for so many years, and to think that someday we might share grandchildren! It does both our hearts good."

Jessica rubbed a hand over her eyes, repressing the urge to weep. "Mom..."

"I don't mean to pressure you."

"I know you don't."

"Good. I'm sorry I woke you, darling. I should have realized you'd be exhausted after this last week. Go back to sleep. We'll talk later."

Sleep was impossible now. Jessica padded barefoot into the kitchen and made coffee, standing at the counter until the liquid had drained into the glass pot. Then she poured herself a mug, and cradling it in both hands, sat at her kitchen table. Balancing her feet against the edge of the chair, her knees propped up under her chin, she waited until the coffee had cooled enough for a first sip. It did little to revive her sagging spirits, settling unsatisfactorily in the pit of her stomach while she mulled over what she was going to do.

Already it had started, already she could feel the ropes tightening around her heart, binding her. She felt imprisoned by what everyone believed was right for her, what everyone believed she wanted herself, when in reality she loved Damian, not Evan.

The phone startled her, and she swore as she spilled coffee on her hands. "Hello," she snapped, grabbing the receiver.

"What the hell's going on?" Cathy demanded, sounding full of righteous indignation.

"Excuse me!" The last thing she needed was her best friend's accusations.

"I picked up the paper this morning, and there's your bright smiling face to greet me."

"So I understand," she muttered.

"There's something wrong with this picture, though. You're with the wrong brother. Care to explain?"

"No."

"Why not?"

Jessica sighed. "It's a long story."

"Condense it."

She sighed again. "Evan's decided to come out of his doldrums—"

"About time, wouldn't you say?"

"Yes, definitely, but he isn't doing this for himself. His father's running for political office and so Evan's making an effort to smile and put on a happy face."

"By dating you."

"It seems so."

"I know all about his father. Walter Dryden's name's been splashed across the headlines all week, right along with Evan's and Earl Kress's," Cathy said impatiently. "So cut to the chase and tell me why you were out on the town with Evan and not Damian."

A simple explanation was beyond Jessica. This was the most complicated misadventure of her life. "You were wrong, Cath," she said miserably. "Damian isn't nearly as fond of me as you assumed. Otherwise he would have said something long before now."

"Said something about what?" Cathy yelped.

"Caring about me," she whispered miserably. She felt as though she was standing chest deep in quicksand with no chance of getting free.

Cathy groaned. "All right, I can see this tale of woe isn't something you're going to be able to abbreviate. Start at the beginning and be sure you tell me everything."

To her credit, Cathy listened attentively to the events of the week, all that had ensued since Jessica's conversation with Evan on Monday morning. When Jessica finished, Cathy was uncharacteristically silent.

"I see what you mean," she said finally, sounding none too happy herself. "Damian's caught between a rock and a hard place. He's crazy about you, Jess. My instincts told me that the day we had lunch."

"But apparently not crazy enough." Jessica closed her eyes to the sharp pain the thought produced.

"Wrong," Cathy corrected defensively. "Damian's got a sense of family and duty so strong he'd sacrifice his own happiness. That's not loving you too little, my friend, that's loving you—and Evan—too damn much."

"If that's the case, then why do I feel like leaping off a bridge? My mother and Lois Dryden are talking about a wedding and grandchildren."

Cathy let the comment pass. "How often do you see Evan?"

"Every day—we work together, remember?"

"I meant socially."

That wasn't a fair question. Because of the trial they'd been together for the better part of each evening, as well as every day. Lunch and dinner had been haphazard affairs while they discussed different aspects of the case and their strategies. It was business, nothing more. He hadn't so much as held her hand.

"We've been seeing a good deal of each other," Jessica said, and then explained.

"I see, and how do you feel about Evan now?"

"I'm glad he's trying to get his life together. But he isn't attracted to me, and doesn't pretend to be, either."

"Then why haven't you said something to Damian? Why haven't you explained?"

"How could I?" Jessica protested tartly. It wasn't that she hadn't thought of doing so a hundred times. "First off, we were both heavily involved in the Earl Kress case. The timing was wrong. I might have said something over dinner last night if Damian had given me any encouragement, but he didn't. I can't help thinking you're wrong about us."

"We've already been through that," Cathy muttered in frustration.

"I know Evan is dating me for show. I wouldn't be surprised if he'd arranged for that photographer himself. It's the sort of thing he'd do."

"Aren't you afraid he'll fall in love with you?"

"No. His heart is so battered it'll be a good long while before he takes a chance on love again."

Cathy was uncharacteristically quiet. "His family's important to him, the same way yours is to you. So play this hand close to your chest, Jess. Vulnerable as he is just now, Evan might develop a deep... affection for you. That would be a disaster."

This was something Jessica had worried about earlier, and she was greatly relieved that their relationship had turned out to be strictly platonic. "You're certainly filled with happy suggestions."

Cathy ignored that, too. "When are you seeing him again?"

"Tomorrow afternoon. He's picking me up for a fund-raiser for his father. It's a picnic." She dreaded the entire affair. If it wasn't for the opportunity of seeing Damian, she'd have found an excuse not to attend.

"Have fun."

"Right," Jessica said, knowing fun would be impossible.

After she'd hung up the phone, Jessica took a shower. She stood under the hard spray, letting the water hammer at her face. When she'd finished she felt better—and filled with purpose.

EVAN ARRIVED to pick her up early the next day. He wore a white sweater with a blue braid along the V-shaped neckline. He looked stylish and debonair, very Ivy League casual. His eyes lit up when he saw her in her cheery summer dress with the short white jacket.

"I can't get over what a beauty you grew up to be."

"You always were a silver-tongued devil," Jessica teased. He was in a good mood, and he had a right to be after the success of the previous week.

Evan's sports car was parked right in front of her building. He held open the door for her and helped her inside. They chatted amiably on the ride to Whispering Willows, where the fund-raising picnic was being held. The area was decorated with banners and American flags, and there was even a small grandstand and a band.

Jessica was determined to find a chance to talk to Damian, to explain her feelings. He couldn't avoid her forever.

Jessica's parents were there, handing out small American flags to the guests. Rows of folding chairs were set up in front of the grandstand for Walter Dryden's speech.

Everyone was busy with one picnic task or another. Jessica helped where she could, keeping her eye out for Damian.

She was busy dishing up potato salad alongside Evan when she first saw Damian. He was talking to an older woman and happened to look in Jessica's direction. Their eyes met for the briefest of seconds before he quickly averted his gaze. Jessica swallowed the pain that constricted her throat.

After the food had been served, Walter Dryden strolled up to Jessica. He was a big man, strong in build and, she knew, equally strong in character. He hugged her and thanked her for all her help.

"You've grown into a beautiful young woman, Jessica." His deep voice echoed what Evan had said to her earlier.

"Thank you. I don't know if I've had a chance to tell you how pleased I am that you've decided to run for senator," she said.

"I wish I'd started my campaign much sooner. I'm going to be stuck playing catch-up the next couple of months, which means a lot of hard work."

"You're exactly what this state needs," Jessica said sincerely.

"Your confidence means a lot to me." They were strolling together side by side. "I've been doing some hard thinking along those lines myself. About how you're exactly what my son needs."

"I'm sorry?"

"You and Evan."

Jessica didn't know what to say. She should have explained then and there that it was Damian she loved, but her throat went dry and her tongue seemed glued to the roof of her mouth.

"He needs you," Walter Dryden repeated.

"He's going to be just fine, Mr. Dryden. I don't think you should worry about him."

Walter Dryden's nod was somber. "Lois and I believe you're responsible for that."

The taste of panic filled her mouth. "I'm sure that's not true."

"Nonsense. You have to learn how to accept a compliment, young lady. It'll serve you well later in life—Evan, too, for that matter." He paused, his look thoughtful. "I believe my son will eventually enter politics himself. He's a natural, but he isn't ready yet and probably won't be for several years. I've had to bite my tongue not to sway that son of mine, but Lois would never forgive me if I pushed him toward something he didn't want."

Jessica hoped he felt the same way about forcing Evan into an unwanted relationship.

"We're getting off the subject," Walter muttered, with a shake of his head. "I wanted to thank you, my dear, for helping Evan."

"But I haven't."

"Nonsense. You've made all the difference in the world to my son these last few weeks. I'd mentioned to Damian that you and I had talked and you'd be coming in for an interview. His decision to hire you was brilliant. I couldn't have thought of anything better for Evan myself."

"I have a lot to thank Damian for," Jessica said, so softly she doubted Walter heard her.

"Ah, here you are," Evan declared, coming up behind them. "Don't tell me my own father is stealing away my favorite girl."

Walter chuckled. "Not likely, son. You two enjoy yourselves now. You've both worked hard all afternoon. Take a break, sneak away and have fun."

"But your speech . . ." Jessica protested.

"No matter. You can hear me speak any day of the week. Now off with you."

Evan reached for her hand, and they walked along the outskirts of the grandstand area. They were moving toward a stand of weeping willow trees, and Jessica found that Evan's mood had changed subtly. He seemed troubled. She waited for him to broach the problem.

"Do you mind if we take a few minutes to talk?" he said after a moment.

"I'd like that." Her heart swelled with relief. What they needed was a healthy dose of honesty. She stopped and leaned against the trunk of a tree. They were partially hidden from view, and the privacy was welcome.

"I don't feel that you and I are connecting, Jessica."

"I know." She thought about her mother and all her talk about a wedding and grandchildren. Her mind drifted back to the conversation she'd had with Evan's father moments earlier. Everything had gone much too far.

"I've wanted to talk to you all week, but everything was so hectic, what with the trial and Dad announcing his candidacy."

"It was quite a week," Jessica agreed.

"Our names have been linked in the newspaper."

"Your name's often in the paper." He was from one of Boston's most prominent families, after all.

Evan chuckled. "That's true enough." He reached for her hand then, holding it between his own. "I'd like all that speculation about us to change. I'm ready to settle down with one woman."

Jessica's heart stopped beating. If he proposed marriage, she swore she was going to break down and weep. Everything and everyone seemed to be working against her, including her own parents.

"I . . . I've always been fond of you, Evan, but I think it's only fair for you to know—"

"'Fond' is such a weak word," he interrupted, frowning.

She didn't want to walk over his already bruised ego. "I know, but—"

"Do you realize we haven't even kissed?" He smiled, his eyes twinkling with boyish eagerness. "That's about to be corrected, sweet Jessica." He placed his hands on both sides of her face and, before she could protest, lowered his mouth to hers.

It was a gentle kiss, undemanding and tender. Jessica felt nothing, except an increasing desire to cry. How could she feel anything for Evan when she cared so deeply for Damian? When she *loved* Damian?

Evan lifted his head from hers and gazed down at her, his eyes now dark and unreadable. He studied her for a moment. "I won't pressure you, Jessica. We'll give this time." He brushed a stray curl from her cheek and kissed her there, his lips warm and moist against her face.

It was then that Jessica saw Damian. He was standing on the edge of the crowd that had gathered to hear Walter's speech. His eyes were on Jessica and Evan. When he realized she'd seen him, he turned and walked away. His steps were brisk and hurried as though he couldn't move fast enough.

For one wild moment, Jessica considered running after him, but Evan had put one arm possessively around her shoulders and was leading her back toward the grandstand.

It was too late.

CHAPTER SEVEN

"WELL?" CATHY DEMANDED without a word of greeting as Jessica opened the apartment door to her friend Sunday evening. Cathy swept her backpack from her shoulder and carelessly tossed it aside. "How'd the picnic go?"

"Politically it was a success. From what I understand, Mr. Dryden raised a lot of money for his campaign." She was avoiding the issue and knew it, but the subject of Evan and Damian had become too painful even to think about.

Cathy knew her well enough to recognize the signs. "Sit down," she instructed, pointing at the overstuffed chair that was Jessica's favorite spot. Her friend became downright dictatorial whenever she felt strongly about something; apparently, she did now.

Jessica followed Cathy's orders simply because she didn't have the force of will to argue. Settling into the chair, she waited while Cathy paced the carpet in front of her. Jessica could almost hear her friend's brain waves crackling.

"I've been giving this matter some thought," Cathy began.

"I can see that," Jessica returned, wondering what Cathy's feverish mind had concocted this time.

"I want you to develop a limp," Cathy said. She sounded as though this was a stroke of pure genius.

Jessica wanted to laugh out loud. "You're joking, right? Because heaven knows I can't take you seriously."

"I'm dead serious, but I only want you to limp when Damian's around, not Evan."

Jessica shook her head, as though that would improve her hearing. For sheer lunacy, this idea ranked right up there with the luncheon invitation. "What possible reason would I have to do something as stupid as fake a limp?"

"Just remember to limp on the same foot," Cathy said, ignoring Jessica's question and looking a bit worried. "This is just the type of thing you'd forget. It might be a good idea if you put a mark on the top of your shoe so you don't goof up."

Jessica held up her hands. "Cathy, have you OD'd on too much sugar or something? This is the craziest thing you've ever suggested!"

"Trust me," Cathy said impatiently. "I'm in theater—I know what I'm doing."

"Your self-confidence doesn't reassure me in the least."

"It should. I know about these things."

"Would it be too much to share the logic of your plan with me?"

"Not at all." Cathy's step was jaunty as she walked over to the sofa, dropped down and crossed her legs. "Sympathy. We want Damian to think you've hurt yourself—a twisted ankle, a trick knee, that sort of thing. If he cares about you half as much as I believe, he won't be able to stand by and do nothing. He'll come to your aid, and the minute he touches you, he won't be able to hide how he feels." She stopped abruptly. "Be warned, though. You should be prepared."

"For what?"

"He might just explode at you. Anger in a man is far more complicated than it is with us women. He'll think you aren't taking care of yourself, and he'll feel responsible for that. Men do that kind of thing, you know. He might even decide to blame Evan, so make sure you take that into account."

"Of course Damian'll get angry!" Jessica cried. "And he'll have every right to be mad once he discovers I'm faking an injury to gain his sympathy."

"Don't let him know that part," Cathy said simply.

"Cathy," Jessica said on the end of a long sigh. "I appreciate your efforts, I really do, but I can't pretend to be hurt. First of all, Damian would know in an instant. I'm not nearly as good an actress as you, and he'd figure out my ploy in no time. You seem to have forgotten Damian's an experienced attorney."

Cathy frowned, chewing on her lower lip as she thought. "Okay," she said after a while. "Forget the limp. The only other thing I can suggest is forthright honesty. You'd be amazed at how well it works sometimes. This might just be one of those times."

"As it happens, I couldn't agree with you more," Jessica said. "This whole situation is preposterous. I'm not any good at charades. I'd like to help Evan, but not at the expense of my emotional well-being."

"Now you're talking." Cathy slid to the edge of the cushion. "What are you going to say to Damian?"

"I . . . don't know yet." A heaviness settled on her shoulders at the thought. "You know what my biggest fear is? That Damian will smile fondly at me and tell me how flattered and honored he is by my little confession."

"With sadness echoing in his voice," Cathy added, demonstrating her usual flair for the dramatic.

"Right. Then he'll sigh and add that unfortunately he doesn't share my feelings."

"That sounds just like a man," Cathy agreed. "Naturally he'll lie through his teeth, because he's being noble for his brother's sake. Just don't listen to him. Trust me, Jess, this guy loves you."

Jessica wished with all her heart that it was true. She looked over to her friend, realizing how much she treasured Cathy's support, and gave her a thumbs-up. Cathy grinned and returned the gesture.

EVAN WAS IN HIS OFFICE working when Jessica arrived Monday morning. "Good morning," he called out cheerfully. "I was hoping it was you."

"Would you like me to put on a pot of coffee?" she asked. Then she glanced toward the machine and noticed Evan had already done so.

He wandered out of his office, mug in hand, and sat on the corner of her desk, one leg swinging like a pendulum. He smiled down on her, his eyes twinkling. "Are you rested and ready to tackle the world?"

Jessica smiled. That didn't describe her even on her best Monday morning. "Not quite. Give me until Wednesday or Thursday for that."

"Then this should help brighten your day," he said casually, withdrawing two tickets from the inside pocket of his jacket and handing them to her. Jessica read the tickets and gasped. "Two box seats for the Red Sox game this evening!"

"I thought you might enjoy baseball."

"I love the Red Sox."

"So your mother told me. Be prepared, Jessica, my lovely, I'm planning to sweep you off your feet."

Her gaze shot up to his. He was sweeping her off her feet all right, but she didn't like where she was landing. She'd awakened that morning determined to resolve this matter between her and the Dryden brothers once and for all, only to be thwarted at the first turn. As if things weren't bad enough, Evan had been conferring with her mother, learning what he could about her.

"Evan, we need to talk," she said, keeping her gaze lowered. All the way into the office she'd practiced what she intended to say.

"I can't now, Jess. Sorry. I'm going to be in court all day with the Porter case. But don't worry, there'll be plenty of time for talking later. I'll come by for you at six-thirty, all right?"

"All right," she muttered, managing a weak smile.

By the time Evan arrived to pick her up that evening, Jessica was determined to have her say—after the game, she decided, when they were afforded some privacy.

Evan was determined, as well, only his determination was to lay on the charm. Their seats were situated directly behind home plate and their view was excellent.

They downed steaming hot dogs, salty peanuts and a glass of draft beer each. Evan was more relaxed than she'd seen him in a long while, cheering on his team and shouting at the umpire. When the Red Sox scored a home run, he placed his fingers in his mouth and let loose with a piercing whistle. In all the years she'd spied on Evan and his brother, she couldn't remember him once whistling like that.

"My mother would've had my hide," he explained when she asked. "Whistling isn't proper behavior," he said, sounding so much like Lois Dryden that Jessica laughed.

"When did that ever stop you?" she teased.

"I found that my yen to whistle was the one thing Dad wouldn't tolerate, either," Evan said, as though cheated out of a normal childhood.

Jessica was amazed. She'd assumed that Evan, who'd always been the fair-haired boy, had gotten away with everything.

In the seventh-inning stretch, Evan reached for her hand and squeezed her fingers. She'd always liked Evan and found it impossible to be irritated with him for any length of time. This was his gift, Jessica realized, what his father had referred to during their talk at the fund-raising picnic. Evan was a born leader. People had always been drawn to him. He'd always been accepted, admired and highly regarded. When uncomfortable situations arose, they viewed him as a problem solver.

Suddenly Jessica felt a change in him. He let her hand slip from his grasp. He stiffened and went utterly still. He gasped, and then seemed to stop breathing altogether.

"Evan?"

His smile was decidedly forced. At that moment the crowd roared and fans got to their feet. Jessica hadn't a clue what had happened in the play. Her eyes and mind were on Evan.

"What's wrong?" she asked when the noise died down.

"Nothing." He attempted to convince her with a smile, but failed. Something was very wrong, indeed, and she was determined to find out what.

"Come on," she said, standing and not waiting for him. "We're leaving."

"Jessica, no, it's all right. I'm fine."

"You're not, and don't even try to tell me otherwise, because I know better."

"It's nothing," he said once more, defensively.

She ignored him, gathered her things and left the box. He had no alternative but to follow her.

"Has anyone ever told you what a stubborn woman you are?" he muttered, racing after her. Their steps echoed against the concrete steps as they made their way out of the stadium. Every now and again they could hear shouts and cheers coming from inside. A couple of times Evan glanced regretfully over his shoulder.

"All right, tell me what happened to you in there," Jessica demanded, as they neared the parking lot.

"It was nothing."

"If you say 'nothing' again, I'm going to scream. Now, who'd you see?" But she already knew the answer. Only one person would have evoked such a pain-filled response in Evan, and that was the woman he'd loved and lost.

"What makes you think I saw anyone?" Evan tossed right back at her, irritated now and not bothering to disguise it.

"Was it Mary Jo?"

He stopped so abruptly she'd taken half a dozen steps before she realized he wasn't at her side.

"Who told you about Mary Jo?" His voice was hoarse.

"No one yet, but you're about to."

"Sorry, Jess, but—"

"Now listen here, Evan Dryden, you need to get this off your chest once and for all. You've nursed the pain she caused you long enough. It's time to let it go. Past time!" Jessica tucked her arm in the crook of his elbow as they wove their way toward his car.

He was silent, his mood dark and brooding by the time they arrived at Jessica's apartment. She wasn't sure if she was helping matters by insisting he tell her about this woman he'd once loved. She feared her insistence might well rip open a half-healed wound, but she also knew he couldn't hold this inside any longer.

Jessica led the way into her kitchen, turned on the light and brewed a pot of coffee. Evan sat down, but grew restless almost immediately and stood, prowling about her small apartment.

Soon Jessica was sitting in her favorite chair, watching Evan pace. She didn't pressure him to talk, didn't try to prompt him. When he was ready, he'd tell her what she wanted to know.

"We met by accident," he said, his voice low and intense, "although I've wondered since if it really was."

"You mean you think she arranged it?"

Evan's eyes widened with surprise. "No...not that. I was thinking that there's little in life that really *is* an accident."

"I see," Jessica murmured.

"I was at the beach with a few friends of mine. We'd played volleyball and had a few beers and were enjoying ourselves—taking a real break from the grind of the office. We soaked up sunshine and laughter and got rid of a lot of pent-up energy."

He stopped moving and turned to face her. "Most of my friends had left and I was winding down by taking a walk along the beach, and that's when I met Mary Jo. She was walking her dog and good old Fighto—bad pun, eh?—anyhow, he got loose. She was chasing him down the beach and, being the heroic kind of guy I am, I caught the leash for her. She stopped to thank me and we got to talking. She's small and pretty with big brown eyes that... Well, none of that matters now."

"You liked her right away?"

Evan nodded. "There was a freshness about her, an enthusiasm that bubbled over. I knew immediately that I wanted to know her better, so I asked her out to dinner. It threw me for a loop when she refused."

That must have been something of a novelty, Jessica mused. "Did she give you a reason?"

"Several, as a matter of fact, but I was able to talk her out of her objections. She had the most marvelous laugh, and I found myself saying the most ridiculous things, just so I could hear it. Being with Mary Jo made me want to laugh myself. It was the most exhilarating day I'd had in years."

"She did go out with you, though?"

"Not exactly." Caught in the memories, Evan didn't seem inclined to say anything more for a minute. Jessica watched silently as the emotions crossed his face. First she saw his eyes light up with the recollection, followed by a pain so deep she yearned to reach out and take his hand. The small movements of his mouth were telling, too. It quivered when he first mentioned meeting Mary Jo, as if that first conversation served to amuse him still. But a moment later, the corners sank as his pain took hold. Jessica longed to reassure him, but knew Evan wouldn't have appreciated it.

"As it happened," Evan continued at last, his tone wistful, "I spent the rest of the day and nearly all of the night with Mary Jo. We built a fire on the beach and talked until morning.

"We started dating regularly after that. I found her refreshing and fun. Our lives were so different. Mary Jo was the youngest of a family of six. She's the only girl. I met her family one Sunday, and her mother insisted I stay for dinner. I'd never seen such a spread in all my life. There were kids running all over the place. Several of Mary Jo's sisters-in-law were pregnant at the time, as well. I've never known such a family, the joking and the teasing and fun. Don't get me wrong, I've got a great family myself, but Mary Jo's is different. I really loved being with them."

"I'm sure they felt the same way about you."

He shrugged, his look doubtful. "I'd like to think so."

"What happened next?" Jessica prompted when he didn't immediately continue. She was eager now for the details.

"I knew I was going to fall in love with her that first day on the beach," he said, his voice so low it was a strain to distinguish the words. "Love isn't something I take lightly, but it hit me then—and I knew."

"I know what you mean," Jessica offered. She felt the same way about Damian.

"After I met her parents, I realized how much I wanted to marry her, how much I wanted us to have five or six children of our own. The Summerhills' home was full of love and I wanted that kind of happy free environment for my own children someday."

"Mary Jo sounds like a very special woman," Jessica said quietly.

"She is," Evan whispered softly. "Special enough to marry."

"You asked her to be your wife, didn't you?"

He gave an odd smile, one that was a blend of amusement and pain. "Yes. Afterward I took her to meet my parents. Mary Jo was intimidated by my family's wealth—I realized that from the beginning. Who wouldn't be, seeing Whispering Willows for the first time. My parents had some doubts about our being suited, but once Mom and Dad met Mary Jo, they changed their minds."

"I don't remember hearing about the engagement," Jessica said.

"I wanted to give her a diamond, but she preferred a pearl ring, instead. She'd recently completed her student teaching and been hired as a first-grade teacher. She wanted to delay making a formal announcement until she'd settled in to her job, but more importantly until after her parents' fortieth wedding anniversary celebration that October.

"I wasn't keen on waiting," Evan confessed, "but I agreed, because, well, because I was willing to do whatever Mary Jo wanted." He paused and drew a deep breath, holding it a moment as if he dreaded continuing. "I first suspected something was wrong the first part of October. She kept finding excuses why we couldn't see one another. In the beginning I accepted them—I was busy myself—and although I missed her, I didn't press the issue. I didn't like it, mind you, but I understood how busy she was with school and her family obligations. A couple of times I showed up at her parents' house. They seemed glad to see me, and her mother obviously assumed I was starving and made me stay for dinner." He smiled.

"They sound like wonderful people."

Jessica didn't think Evan heard her. "When Mary Jo mailed me back the ring, I was stunned. I've had some surprises in my life, both pleasant and unpleasant, but none that have shocked me more."

Jessica felt angry at Mary Jo for not having the courage to confront Evan face-to-face. If she wanted to break the engagement, even an informal one, then the least she could have done was have the consideration to tell him in person. Mailing Evan the ring was cowardly and cruel.

"So," Evan continued, "I drove over to her apartment in a fury."

"You had every right to be furious."

He shook his head. "I should have waited until I'd cooled down. I wish with everything in me that I had."

Life was filled with regrets, Jessica thought. She'd been carrying around a fair share of her own, especially in the past few weeks.

"When I confronted her, Mary Jo told me there was someone else," he whispered. "I didn't believe her at first. I refused to entertain the thought that a woman as fundamentally honest as Mary Jo would see another man behind my back. It didn't tally in my mind—but I was wrong." His voice dwindled to a whisper. "Apparently they met at the school where she teaches. He's a teacher, too. The agony of being engaged to me and in love with someone else must have torn her apart."

Jessica dropped her gaze for fear he would read what was in her eyes. She wasn't engaged to Evan, but she continued to see him when she was in love with Damian. While Evan spoke, Jessica had been casting mental stones at Mary Jo, when she was guilty of essentially the same thing.

"You saw her tonight at the ball game?" Jessica gently prodded.

Evan nodded. "She was with him...at least I assume it was him." The pain was back in his eyes, and Jessica felt the urge to weep. For Evan, yes, but for herself, as well. What a couple they made, each in love with someone else, fighting hard to do the right thing and making themselves miserable in the process.

"Mary Jo's a special woman," Evan whispered. "The man who marries her is a lucky man..." He paused again, and that odd smile, the one of blended joy and pain returned. "She'll be a wonderful wife and mother."

"Under the circumstances, that's a generous thing to say."

"You don't know Mary Jo, or you'd think the same thing yourself. In the months since we parted, I've come to realize that my ego played a substantial role in all this. Mary Jo was the first woman to break off a relationship with me." He smiled as he said it, as though it had served him right after all these years. "I guess I'd gotten a bit cocky."

"We're all guilty of that in one form or another," she offered.

He looked at Jessica then, and his gaze sobered. "I've ruined our evening, haven't I?"

"No," she told him, hoping he heard the sincerity in her voice. She understood how passionately Evan had loved the woman, and how deeply the pain of their parting affected him still.

More than ever, after hearing Evan talk about losing the woman he loved, Jessica knew she couldn't allow the same thing to happen to her. She couldn't continue to mislead Evan by letting him believe their relationship would evolve into something it was never meant to be.

A WEEK PASSED. Every time she was with Evan he told her more about his relationship with Mary Jo. She soon realized that every invitation to dinner or a show was an excuse to talk. Every outing was followed by coffee and a long heart-to-heart. It was as though a floodgate had opened inside him, and the need to release the pent-up emotion was too strong to ignore.

They were friends, nothing more, and Jessica was comfortable with their relationship. With their frequent talks, she was able to open up to him, as well, in little ways.

"Have you ever been in love, Jessica?" he asked her unexpectedly one night.

"I think so," she said hesitantly as they strolled through Boston Common. "Yes," she amended quickly. "And it isn't what you're thinking."

"Oh?"

"It's not you, so don't get a big head." She didn't realize until she spoke how insulting she sounded, and she immediately sought his pardon.

Evan laughed off her apology.

The night was lovely. The stars were like twinkling rows of sequins that hung so close they seemed draped over the upper limbs of the trees.

"You know when it's love, don't you?" he asked after a few moments.

"Oh, yes," she whispered.

"Does this mystery man feel the same way about you?"

"I...I don't know. I like to think so." Although there were more signs to the contrary.

For Damian continued to avoid her. Other than that brief moment when he'd come into her office, she hadn't talked to him once.

He arrived at the office promptly at eight each morning and left at five. She guessed that his involvement with his father's campaign dictated his hours. That meant if she wanted to see him, it had to be during working hours. With his hectic schedule it was easier getting an audience with the pope. Jessica didn't know how Damian managed to cram all he did into a single workday. She'd tried to talk to him, but hadn't found the opportunity when there weren't other people around.

Jessica was fast losing her patience. And then, just when she was about to throw her hands in the air and scream with frustration, it happened. Quite by accident, and where she'd least expected it.

Whispering Willows. His family's home.

Evan had learned from Jessica's mother that she'd played on her college tennis team; he'd been intrigued, and challenged her to a game. It had sounded like an entertaining way to spend a Saturday afternoon, and she'd agreed. Since he'd neglected to schedule time on the courts at the country club, they drove to his parents' home to play.

They smacked the ball back and forth for a solid hour, and Evan soundly defeated her. Not that his athletic ability surprised her, but in her effort to impress him she strained her knee. It wasn't anything serious, but Evan insisted they stop playing.

They made their way to the house, laughing and in a good mood, her knee long forgotten, to discover Evan's mother anxiously attempting to start her car, without success. She needed to be at campaign headquarters within the hour and was fretting about what she should do.

"Not to worry, Mom," Evan said, affectionately kissing his mother's cheek. "I'll drive you."

"Nonsense," Lois protested when she viewed Evan's two-seater sports car.

"Didn't you tell me you gave Richmond the day off?" Evan said, opening his car door. "No more excuses, Mom."

"But what about Jessica?"

"I'm perfectly capable of entertaining myself," Jessica assured her. She stood in the driveway until the car had disappeared, then wandered back into the house, wiping the perspiration from her brow with the back of her forearm. She walked into the kitchen and, finding a cold soda in the refrigerator, helped herself.

She was humming a show tune when the kitchen door swung open. "Mother, what in blazes are you doing here? You're supposed to be at—" Damian stopped when he saw her. "Jessica," he said, his surprise evident.

"Your mother's car wouldn't start, so Evan drove her over to campaign headquarters," she explained. Her face was red with exertion, and her hair fell in damp tendrils about her face.

"Evan drove her." Already Damian was physically withdrawing from her. "I'd better go see what's wrong with Mom's car."

"Damian..." Cathy's suggestion about faking an injury came into her mind like a stone from a slingshot. She was injured—well, only slightly—but there was no better time than the present to make use of it.

She concentrated her efforts on her right foot and limped toward him. She hated resorting to such an underhanded method but she was desperate to talk to him. Surely he'd forgive her once he learned the truth.

His gaze went to her knee, his concern immediate. She was wearing a white top and a short tennis skirt. "You hurt yourself," he said, moving toward her. The kitchen door swung in his wake.

"I'm fine," she whispered.

"Sit down," he ordered, his voice none too tender. "Does Evan know about this?"

"Yes, but it's not all that bad," she mumbled. He pulled out a kitchen chair and eased her into it. His hands at her shoulders were gentle but firm. She closed her eyes at his touch. Lord, how she'd missed him! For days she'd waited for the opportunity to be alone with Damian, and she wasn't about to waste it now.

"We need to talk," she said. "Listen, I—"

"We'll talk after I've seen to your knee. What in God's name possessed my brother to leave you like this?"

"Damian, please listen to me."

"Later." He was busy at work packing ice into a bag.

She was irritated now and leapt off the chair. "My knee will be fine. I strained a muscle or something. It's no big deal."

"You'd better have a doctor check it out," he insisted, positioning her back in the chair, raising her leg and resting it against the seat of a second chair, then balancing the ice pack on the knee.

"I need to talk to you about Evan and me," she said, refusing to be put off any longer. "I'm not in love with Evan and he doesn't love me. We're friends, nothing more. He's in love with Mary Jo and I'm in love with—"

"Keep that ice pack on your leg for a good twenty minutes, understand?"

Infuriated, Jessica rose to her feet and tossed the ice pack into the sink. "You're going to listen to me, Damian, if it kills me! I realize I'm making a mess of this. I should never have used my knee to keep you here, but I was desperate."

"Did you or did you not twist your knee?" he demanded.

"Yes, a little, but it's nothing. I want to talk about the two of us. About you and me."

"Jessica," he said with ill-concealed impatience. "You're dating my brother."

"Your brother and I are *friends,* nothing more. How many times do I have to say it?"

"There's a change in Evan," Damian insisted heatedly. "Do you think I haven't noticed? For the first time in months, he's his old self. My brother's back again and it's all due to you."

"Maybe, Damian, but not in the way you think."

"It doesn't matter what I think," Damian said angrily. "You're dating my brother, so there can't be a you and me. Do you understand?"

"No!" she cried. "No, I don't!"

"It has to be this way, Jessica."

"But why?" Hot tears blurred her vision.

He didn't answer her for several time-shattering seconds. "That's just the way it is."

"Is . . . is that the way you want it?" Swallowing became impossible. She knotted her hands into fists at her sides.

"Yes," he said after a moment, the longest moment of her life. "That's the way I want it."

Jessica turned away from him, grateful to the very depths of her soul that she hadn't declared her undying love for him. This humiliation was bad enough.

"Jessica." Her name was a plea on his lips.

She hung her head, knowing he would abandon her the way he always did—but he didn't. Instead, his arms came around her and turned her to face him. His touch was as if he had to experience holding her, as if the feel of her was the one thread keeping his sanity intact. And then his mouth came down on hers.

This kiss was hungry and hard, unlike the kisses they'd shared previously. Jessica clung to him, mindful only of this man and the sheer joy she experienced in his arms. She caressed his face with wondering fingers as the intensity of their need increased. He angled her head to one side for a series of short nibbling kisses down her cheek, her throat.

"No more," he moaned, then jerked his head away. But she refused to release him, hugging him around the neck and burying her face in his shoulder. "Jessica, please." When he tugged her hands free, she realized he was shaking as badly as she was. His hands closed around hers and his head fell forward.

The sound of the front door closing echoed like a clap of thunder. Damian moved away from her and had his back to her when Evan strolled into the kitchen, whistling. He stopped when he saw Damian.

"Damian, hello. I'm glad to see you kept my best girl company."

With something less than a curt nod to his brother, Damian strode out of the kitchen, muttering about seeing to his mother's car.

Jessica thought her heart would break.

CHAPTER EIGHT

"THANK YOU," Evan said when he dropped Jessica off at her apartment half an hour later. "By the way, there's a formal dinner with three hundred of my father's closest friends Monday night," he said casually. "I'd like you to attend it with me."

Jessica looked up at Evan, realizing she hadn't heard what he'd said. She hurt too much. Damian didn't love her, didn't want her. She'd all but blurted out her love for him, and he'd rejected her, insisted Evan needed her, and then walked away. As he always did.

"Jessica, are you all right?"

"I'm fine." How easily the lie came, even though she was falling apart on the inside.

"I was asking you about the dinner party."

She blinked. Dinner party?

"Monday night," he said slowly, waving a hand in front of her face. "You'd better tell me what's wrong."

"Would it be all right if I go in now?" she asked, instead. She wasn't in the mood to explain anything, least of all what had happened between her and Damian.

"Of course."

Evan insisted on escorting her into her apartment. He placed her tennis racket in the hall closet and stepped into her kitchen to get her a glass of ice water.

Jessica sat at the table and smiled her appreciation. "I'm fine," she said, and this time it was a little less of a lie. Yes, she hurt but it was a clean cut, deep and swift. She knew now what she'd suspected all along. Damian didn't want her, didn't love her.

"Thank you, Jess," Evan said again, and although his words were casual, Jessica sensed a deeper meaning.

"For letting you whop me in tennis?" she asked, knowing it was much more than that.

The smile faded from his eyes. "For that, too, but mostly for listening to me these last few days. Talking about Mary Jo has helped clear my head. It's shown me what went wrong between us and helped me realize how much I still love her." This was issued with a pain-filled sigh.

"That isn't a sin, Evan." Any more than her loving Damian was a sin.

"Talking is what's helped me. Perhaps you should take note and tell me what's troubling you. You can't fool me—those are tears glistening in your eyes."

Instinctively she lowered her gaze, focusing her attention on the water glass. "I . . . I'm not ready to talk just yet. Don't be upset with me. I have to sort through my own feelings first."

His hand covered hers. "I understand. You will attend the dinner party with me, won't you?"

Jessica's first inclination was to refuse. Instead, she nodded. "All right." Sitting home feeling sorry for herself would solve nothing. Nor would she give Damian the satisfaction. From here on out, she was going to kick up her heels and enjoy life. Even if it killed her, and that was what it felt like just now.

"Damian will be there," Evan said as if he expected her to comment.

She nodded. After this afternoon it made no difference.

"He'll be bringing someone, too," Evan added. "You won't mind if we share a table, will you?"

"I won't mind in the least," Jessica said brightly. "The more the merrier."

"I THOUGHT WE'D LOOK through your wardrobe before dinner," Cathy said as she entered Jessica's apartment. Jessica realized her mistake the moment she'd mentioned the dinner party to her friend. From that point on, Cathy had insisted she choose the dress.

"I've managed to dress myself without a problem for several years now," Jessica felt obliged to say.

Cathy was sorting through the dresses in her closet, shuffling them from one side to another as if this was a mission of great importance. She paused and tapped her foot impatiently. "I can't tell you how disappointed I am in Damian. You're sure you didn't misunderstand him?" She sounded as though the fault was Jessica's.

"There was no misunderstanding," Jessica said firmly, wishing she'd never mentioned the incident to Cathy. She wouldn't have except that her friend had been on virtually every phase of this…this mess. "He doesn't want anything to do with me. He couldn't have made it any plainer."

"I don't believe it. There's something very wrong here, and it's up to you to figure out what it is."

"I know what it is," Jessica protested. It wasn't necessary to dissect the problem when the answer was so simple. If Damian *did* care for her, he would have found a way to make things right. He didn't, and he hadn't.

"You're coming to my opening night, aren't you?" Cathy asked as she continued to examine the contents of Jessica's closet.

"I wouldn't miss it for the world." Jessica was proud of Cathy's big career break. She'd gotten the plum role of Adelaide, after all, in the local production of *Guys and Dolls*. Jessica also thought Cathy was sweet on the director, David Carson. Her friend had mentioned his name several times in passing, and Jessica thought there'd been a small catch in her voice each time.

"I think I'll invite Damian to my opening," Cathy suggested nonchalantly. "After all, I have met him."

Jessica wasn't likely to forget. Cathy's eyes shifted in her direction. "You don't have anything to say."

"Do what you want, Cathy."

Cathy's laugh was short and telling. "You can't fool me, Jess, I know you too well. I don't know what's wrong with Damian, but trust me, he'll soon come around."

"I sincerely doubt it." Jessica hated to be so pessimistic, but she couldn't stop herself.

Cathy took three dresses from the closet and laid them across her friend's bed. Her hands on her hips, she circled the bed, then returned two of the dresses to the closet.

Jessica studied Cathy's selection. It was a full-length black dress, sleek and shiny with silver highlights that sparkled in the overhead light.

"Try it on," Cathy insisted.

Mumbling her discontent, Jessica slipped out of her clothes and into the dress, lifting her hair so Cathy could close the zipper properly. Then she regarded herself in the full-length mirror. Her shoulders drooped as she released a slow, defeated sigh.

"I look like Natasha from the Rocky and Bullwinkle cartoon show," she muttered.

"Nonsense," Cathy said. "The dress is perfect."

"For consorting with spies maybe," Jessica muttered. But then again, maybe it *was* right. If she was destined to sit at the same table as Damian and his date, she wanted to be darn sure he noticed her—and knew what he was missing.

EVAN ARRIVED to pick her up for the dinner party five minutes ahead of schedule, just as Jessica was putting the finishing touches to her makeup. "Beautiful," he said, taking both her hands in his. "You're absolutely beautiful."

His appreciation lent Jessica confidence—until they reached the table where Damian and his date were sitting. The woman was tall, regal, blond and gorgeous. Every woman's basic nightmare. So much for the best-laid plans.

"Nadine Powell," Damian said. "My brother, Evan, and Jessica Kellerman."

Jessica's gaze moved to Damian, and she was gratified to discover he was staring at her the way a child gazes into a store window at Christmastime. Cathy had been right—the dress was perfect. Damian abruptly looked away as if angry with himself for being so obvious.

"Nadine," Evan said, taking the other woman's hand and holding it several moments longer than necessary.

Dinner was a drawn-out affair, with speeches from several long-winded politicians. Jessica lost count of the number of speakers and the number of courses served, but they seemed to be running neck and neck. The speeches made dinner conversation almost impossible, but Jessica did manage to learn that Nadine was a longtime friend of Damian's. Friends and nothing more, Nadine went on to explain, reading the situation with amazing accuracy. As for Damian, well, he pretended she wasn't there. He didn't say one word to her the entire meal.

When the dessert dishes were removed, a ten-piece orchestra began to play on a low stage behind the polished oak dance floor.

"You game?" Evan asked, holding out his hand to Jessica. The music was from the forties, the big-band sound she particularly loved. Evan was tapping his foot and swaying his shoulders.

Jessica declined. She wasn't keen on being one of the first ones on the floor. "I think I'd prefer to sit out a few of the numbers, if you don't mind."

"Nonsense. I won't take no for an answer." Evan all but pulled her out of her chair. He led her onto the dance floor, and although the number was fast, he brought her into his arms and held her close.

"Evan," she hissed, acutely aware of the impression they were creating. It looked as if they were madly in love and couldn't bear to be separated.

"Shh," he whispered close to her ear.

"What's wrong with you?"

"Me?" he asked, then threw back his head and laughed as if she'd said something uproariously funny.

"Nothing. I'm having a good time, that's all."

"At my expense," she told him in an angry whisper. "Soon everyone will be talking about us."

"Let them."

"Something is very wrong," Jessica insisted.

He laughed again. "Not exactly, but soon everything should be just right."

Jessica hadn't a clue what he meant, but she wasn't going to continue with this farce any longer than necessary. As soon as the number finished, she broke away from him and returned to their table.

"Jessica's knee is bothering her," Evan explained, and before she realized what was happening, Evan had asked Nadine to dance and the pair stood and left the table. Damian looked unnerved.

"Well," Jessica said dryly, "I guess you can't keep a good man down."

Damian frowned darkly. "He might have asked someone other than my date." His hand closed around his water glass, and he seemed intent on studying the dancing couples. Intent on not making conversation with her, Jessica thought, which was fine. Just fine. Everything had already been said as far as she could see, and apparently Damian felt the same way.

"How's your knee?" Damian asked unexpectedly.

"It's okay. Evan was using it as an excuse to dance with Nadine."

The music circled them in a warm halo of melody. Soon Jessica was tapping her foot, wishing she hadn't been so quick to insist she leave the dance floor.

"Come on," Damian said with a decided lack of enthusiasm. He stood and offered her his hand.

Stunned, Jessica looked up at him.

"There's nothing worse than sitting with a woman who obviously wants to dance."

"I..." She intended to tell him there was nothing worse than dancing with someone who obviously didn't want to be her partner. But before she could speak, he'd taken her hand. He was muttering something under his breath, which she couldn't quite make out. She did hear Evan's name, and she guessed he wasn't pleased with his brother.

Jessica wanted to kick Evan for leaving her alone with Damian. The orchestra had been playing fast-paced songs, but when Damian and Jessica moved onto the floor, the band began a slow dreamy number. The lights lowered and Jessica groaned inwardly.

"Let's sit this one out," she suggested.

"Not on your life," Damian said, easing her into his arms. She didn't understand why he felt obliged to dance with her. He held her stiffly in his arms as though afraid to bring her close. His back was rigid and he stared straight ahead.

"Relax," he whispered impatiently. "I won't bite."

"Me?" she said. "I might as well be waltzing with a mannequin."

"Okay, let's both make an effort."

Jessica hadn't realized she was so tense. Determined to do as he suggested, she closed her eyes and released a slow sigh. She felt the tension ease from Damian, and when she opened her eyes he'd brought her closer, close enough for her to rest her temple against the side of his jaw. The solace she found, as their bodies swayed gently to the rhythm, was worth every minute she'd waited to feel his arms around her.

This was where she belonged, Jessica mused sadly, where she'd always belonged. Surely Damian felt it too. Why else would he be holding her as if she was the most precious thing in his world? Why else would his lips be moving against her hair as if he longed to kiss her.

Neither spoke, she realized, because they feared words would destroy the moment. She clung to him even when the music stopped, not wanting this blissful time to end.

"We should get back to the table," Damian said, and the reluctance she heard in his voice gave her hope.

"I don't see Evan or Nadine. Do you want to dance one more number?" she asked.

He didn't answer her for a long moment, and then said gruffly, "Yes."

"I do, too."

"Jessica, listen . . ."

She chanced raising her face and looking at him, her eyes filled with a longing so great she couldn't hide it. Pressing her finger over his mouth, she smiled. "Please, Damian, not now."

He briefly closed his eyes, sighed and nodded.

Jessica lost track of time. She knew they danced far longer than they should have, for more numbers than she could count. Every once in a while she glanced at their table, but neither Nadine or Evan were in sight.

It wasn't until the music sped up again, that he revealed any signs of regret. She knew something was wrong the minute he eased her from his arms. His face hardened. She looked up at him and blinked, not understanding.

"I'll have my brother's hide for this," Damian muttered.

"For what?" she asked softly.

A muscle in his jaw jerked as he reined in his temper, but that was the only answer she got.

They left the dance floor and sat like strangers at the table. Jessica couldn't bear it any longer. She stood, excused herself and moved from table to table to greet several old family friends. She returned only when she saw that Evan had joined his brother. Nadine was nowhere in sight. The two brothers seemed to be having a rapid intense exchange of words, but when she approached, Damian clamped his mouth closed and looked the other way.

"I've neglected you," Evan said contritely, claiming her hand between both of his. "I'm sorry, Jessica. Can you forgive me?"

"Of course." What else could she do? Demand that he immediately take her home? That would have been silly. Especially as she wasn't interested in him as anything other than a friend. Besides, his neglect had given her all that time with Damian.

A breathless and laughing Nadine returned to the table a few moments later, and the four of them ordered drinks. The waitress had just brought their order when Walter and Lois Dryden approached their table.

"I hope you four are enjoying yourselves."

Evan said that they certainly had been.

Lois smiled benevolently down on Jessica, then gently placed her hands on Jessica's shoulders, leaning forward so that their heads were close together. "We owe you so much," she said, kissing her cheek.

"Nonsense." The words embarrassed her.

"It's true. Tell her, Walter," Lois insisted. "We were about to despair over what was happening with Evan, and that all changed the minute you started working for the firm."

"Mother..." Evan didn't seem to appreciate this, either.

"It's true. You have no idea how pleased Joyce and I are that the two of you are seeing so much of each other," Lois continued.

"I have to agree with your mother," Walter said in his deep, vibrant voice. "You're a good man, Evan, with a bright future. It was a damn shame to watch you waste your life over a woman you couldn't have. It's much better now that you're seeing Jessica."

A stilted uncomfortable silence followed his father's praise. Within a few minutes of the elder Drydens' visit to their table, Damian made an excuse, and he and Nadine got up and left. After that, Evan didn't seem too keen to stay, either. As for Jessica, she was more than happy to get home. Enough was enough.

SHE LAY AWAKE most of the night thinking, and by daybreak, she'd made her decision. With purpose driving her steps, Jessica walked into the office the next morning, her eyes burning from lack of sleep.

"I need to see Mr. Dryden for a moment," she told Damian's secretary.

The woman, doubtless noting the determination in Jessica's voice, reached instantly for the intercom and announced her.

Jessica strode into Damian's office and stood before him. He was sitting behind his desk reading a file. He glanced up, his expression, as always, inscrutable. "What can I do for you, Jessica?"

Her heart pounding, she said flatly, "I'm resigning from my position with this firm, effective immediately." It was an impulsive thing to do, Jessica realized, considering how difficult it was these days to find a job. But her sanity was more important. She'd do temporary work if she had to. Or work in another field.

If Damian was surprised by her announcement, he didn't reveal it. He leaned back in his chair, calm and composed. "This is rather sudden, isn't it?"

"Yes...but it's necessary." She avoided eye contact by studying the painting on the wall behind him. It was a seascape with the ocean crashing against the jagged edge of a protruding rock. A bird was perched on the uppermost point of the rock, undisturbed by the raging sea. Jessica wished she could be more like that bird.

"Does Evan know?"

"Not yet," she replied. "Since you were the one to hire me, I felt obligated to tell you first."

He paused as if gathering his thoughts. "If you could work out your two-week notice, I'd appreciate it."

Jessica wasn't sure what she'd expected. Nothing, she'd told herself, but she realized now that wasn't true. In the deepest part of her, she was praying Damian would ask her to reconsider, that he'd make at least one attempt to change her mind. Perhaps a raise or some other inducement. Instead, he calmly accepted her resignation as if he was almost pleased to see her go.

That hurt. She held the pain to herself for as long as she could, before turning and walking toward the door.

"Jessica."

She stopped, but didn't turn around.

"You've been a valuable asset to this firm, and we'll miss you."

That was all he was willing to offer. It was damn little.

"Thank you," she whispered, then walked out the door.

She was trembling by the time she sat down at her own desk. After taking a moment to compose herself, she reached for the phone and dialed Cathy's number.

"You did *what?*" her friend cried.

Jessica had never used the office phone for personal calls before, but she made this day the exception. "You heard me. I quit."

"But why?"

"It's a long story," she murmured, "but suffice to say, I'm tired of this whole ridiculous charade."

"Damian loves you."

"No," she whispered, "he doesn't." She'd been swayed by Cathy's comments and her own foolish heart, because she so desperately wanted to believe it was true.

"Jessica, Jessica, Jessica," Cathy said in an impatient singsong, "don't be so hasty."

It was either leave the firm or lose her sanity, Jessica mused. It'd been a mistake to contact Cathy; her friend simply didn't understand.

"What did Evan say?"

"He doesn't know yet," she admitted reluctantly. Not that it would make any difference. No argument Evan offered could convince her to change her mind.

"Keep me informed, will you? Following what's going on in your life is more interesting than my soap operas."

Mrs. Sterling came into the office and stared at Jessica, looking as if she were about to burst into tears. "You're leaving!"

This office had an information network the CIA would envy. Jessica didn't bother to ask where Evan's secretary had heard the news; it didn't matter.

"But you can't go now, not when Mr. Dryden's back to his old self."

"I apologize for leaving you in the lurch."

"You won't reconsider?"

Jessica shook her head.

"Personally," said Mrs. Sterling, "I think it makes for bad politics when men and women from the same office date one another. These things have a way of turning sour."

"What does?" Evan asked, stepping into the room, carrying a leather briefcase and looking very much the professional he was. He paused at his secretary's desk and reached for his mail.

"Jessica's resigned," Mrs. Sterling said baldly.

Evan dropped the mail and turned to stare at Jessica. His mouth fell open with disbelief. "Is it true?"

She nodded. Until she saw the look of dismay on his face, she hadn't believed he held any real affection for her.

"Come into my office," he commanded, leading the way and clearly expecting her to follow. When she was inside, he closed the door.

"What's this all about?" he demanded.

To the best of her memory, Jessica had never seen this side of Evan. He looked and acted like Damian. "It's time I moved on," she said weakly, not knowing exactly how much to say, if anything, about the real reason.

"After less than two months?"

She crossed her arms and shrugged.

"Are the hours too long?"

"No."

"We're not paying you enough?"

"I'm receiving an adequate salary," she returned. She didn't like the way he was putting her on the defensive, and she stiffened her resolve. There was a side of her he hadn't seen, either—her stubborn side.

"There must be a reason you find it so repugnant to work for me."

"I never said I found it repugnant to work for you." She dropped her hands and formed tight fists at her sides. Evan was acting every inch the attorney.

"So it's the firm you don't like. Have we done something to offend you?"

"No!" she cried, hating this interrogation. Evan's reaction was certainly the opposite of Damian's. Evan was clearly upset at the idea of losing her.

"Then why? You owe me an explanation," he insisted.

"I don't feel I do..." She hesitated, her stomach in knots.

"Is it something I've done?" His voice was gentler now, as if he was trying to soothe her, to gain her confidence.

"No," she assured him. "You've been wonderful...a good friend. I'll treasure the times we've had together, Evan, but you don't love me and I don't love you. It seems to me that we should appreciate what we do share and not try to make something of it that isn't there." Or allow their parents to do so, either, she added mentally.

He looked puzzled. "That's no reason to quit working for the firm."

"Perhaps not, but it's the right thing for me. Damian asked me to work out my two-week notice, which I'll gladly do, but I'm not going to change my mind."

"All right," he agreed reluctantly. "In the meantime, you don't mind if we continue to see one another, do you?"

"I'm...not sure it would be wise."

Evan jerked back his head as though her answer amazed him. "You aren't serious, are you?"

"Yes, Evan, I am. I enjoy your company and consider you a friend, but..."

"What about coffee to talk over old times?"

"Perhaps."

Evan grinned then, that devilishly handsome grin guaranteed to stir the heart of any woman. "I'm not letting you back out of our sailing date, though. I've been counting on that. You aren't going to let me down, are you?"

"No, I won't let you down." Nevertheless, Jessica's heart sank as she remembered her promise to go out with Evan on his sailboat in three weeks' time. He'd made the date *before* the formal dinner event. *Before* she'd known she wanted out of the Drydens' sphere.

He beamed her a wide smile.

Jessica stayed late that night, wanting to clear her desk before she headed back to her apartment. Undaunted by her stated reluctance to continue seeing him socially, Evan had asked her to dinner, and Jessica had declined. Besides, she'd been out late the night before, hadn't slept well and was anxious to finish up at the office and head back to her apartment.

She was leaving just as Damian came out of his office.

"Good night," she said cordially, moving down the corridor to wait for the elevator. Damian joined her there.

The doors opened and they stepped inside together. They stood like strangers while the elevator made its descent. Jessica stared at the numbers above the door as they lighted up one by one. Only a week earlier, she would have been thrilled to have these few seconds alone with Damian, and now she would have given anything to avoid him. Being this close to him physically and so far apart emotionally was agony in its purest form.

The elevator doors silently slid open, and Jessica stepped into the lobby, glad to make her escape. Damian would go about his life, and she would go about hers.

"Jessica." Damian sounded impatient, but she didn't know if it was with her or himself. "Are you taking the subway?"

"Yes, it's right around the corner." She began to move away.

"I'll give you a ride home."

"No, thank you."

"I insist," Damian said in steel tones. "It's time we talked."

If Jessica had thought her heart was beating hard that morning when she entered his office, it didn't compare with the way it thundered against her ribs now.

Silently he led her into the parking garage to his car. He unlocked the passenger-side door and held it open for her, then went around to the driver's side and climbed in. As he inserted the key into the ignition, he asked, "Have you spoken to Evan about your resignation?"

"Yes."

"What did he have to say?"

She gestured weakly with her hands. "He asked me to reconsider."

"Have you?"

"No. I'll work out my two-week notice, since you asked me to, but my decision stands."

Damian's hands tightened around the steering wheel. "Why, Jessica?"

"Why should you care, Damian?" she returned, losing patience with him. "This morning, you couldn't wait to be rid of me."

"That's not true," he said sharply.

"I don't think discussing this will solve anything," she said, reaching for the door handle, intent on letting herself out.

The air was electric. "Jessica, stay for a few minutes. Please." His words were soft, without emotion, and yet filled with it.

Jessica hesitated. "All right." She dropped her hand.

"Did you give your notice because of what happened at the dinner?" he asked.

Confused, Jessica turned to study Damian. "Last night?"

"Evan virtually abandoned you. I know your feelings must have been hurt, but—"

"Just a minute," she said, twisting in her seat to look at him directly. "You don't honestly believe that, do you?"

A puzzled look crowded his features. "Yes. My brother was rude in the extreme to abandon you the way he did."

She was angrier than she could remember being in a long time. When she let things fester inside her this way, her anger took the form of hiccups when she released it.

"Do you think *hic* I'm so shallow I'd quit *hic* my job in a fit of *hic* jealousy? Is that *hic* what you're saying, Damian?"

He blinked when she was finished, as though he expected more.

Jessica threw open the car door, climbed out and slammed it. "I *hic* don't think this *hic* conversation is getting us anywhere."

With that she marched away. She thought she heard Damian's car door close, but she didn't bother to look back.

"Jessica!" he called storming into the empty lobby.

She hesitated. The hiccups hadn't subsided, and she was having a hard time breathing properly.

"I'm sorry," he said after a tense moment.

She understood then. He was apologizing for much more than their argument. He was telling her how much he regretted not loving her.

CHAPTER NINE

OTHER THAN BRIEF GLIMPSES Jessica didn't see Damian at all during the next two weeks. A new legal assistant, Peter McNichols, was hired, and Jessica helped train the conscientious young man.

On her last day, Damian sent word that he wanted to see her in his office. Mrs. Sterling issued the summons. "I hope you'll change your mind," Evan's secretary said wistfully. "You're an excellent worker and I hate to see you go." She cast a speculative eye toward Evan's closed office door. "I'm sure Mr. Dryden's going to miss you, too."

Evan had made several attempts in the past two weeks to bribe her into staying, but Jessica had stood steadfastly by her decision. Although it had been made impulsively, it was the right thing to do.

Jessica reached for her pad and pen before starting toward Damian's office, although she doubted he expected her to take notes. She was promptly shown in by his secretary.

She found Damian standing at the window, his back to her. His hands were clasped behind him, the pose he assumed when he was thinking or when he was troubled about something. She wondered if he found her departure distressing, then decided if that was the case he'd have said so long before now.

"You wanted to see me?" she asked quietly.

He turned around and offered her a reassuring smile. "Yes, please sit down." He motioned toward the chair, then claimed the seat behind his desk. He reached for an envelope on the corner and handed it to Jessica.

"It's your paycheck," he explained. "I took the liberty of adding a small bonus."

"That wasn't necessary," she said, surprised by the gesture.

"Perhaps not, but I wanted you to know how much the firm appreciated the extra time and effort you put into the Earl Kress case."

"I stayed late because I wanted to."

"I realize that. Now," he said, leaning back in his chair, his posture casual, his eyes curious, "have you found another position yet?"

"No." Working every day had made searching for a job almost impossible. There would be time enough for that later, in the days and weeks to follow.

"I see," he said unemotionally. "If you like, I'd be happy to write you a letter of recommendation."

The offer was generous in light of the fact she'd worked for the firm such a short while.

"I'd appreciate that very much." She'd given considerable thought to the consequences of being out of a job. A letter of recommendation would help.

"There are a number of firms I know who might be interested in obtaining a top-notch legal assistant. I could make a few calls on your behalf."

Damian was being more than generous, she thought. "Thank you. I'd be grateful."

He nodded and she got to her feet. Saying goodbye to Damian was much more difficult than she'd ever expected. When she walked out the door she didn't know how long it'd be before she saw him again. Their families might be close, but Jessica and Damian led very separate lives. It could well be months or even years before they ran into each other. But perhaps that would be for the best. She fidgeted with the yellow notepad. "I want you to know how much I've appreciated working for you and Evan," she said, barely managing to keep her voice steady. "You were willing to give me a chance when all I had was classroom experience."

"You've proved yourself in countless ways since then."

She backed away, taking small steps, until her back was against his door. She felt the wood pressing against her shoulder blades. "Thank you, too," she said, and her voice came out a hoarse whisper, "for everything else."

His brow creased with a frown.

"For the dinners and our time at Cannon Beach," she elaborated. The final words stuck in her throat, and she was sure that if she said what was really in her heart, it would embarrass them both.

His eyes revealed his sadness. "Goodbye, Jessica."

She turned then and opened the door, but before she walked out of his life, before she took that first step, she glanced over her shoulder to look once again, to grab hold of this last memory of him.

Damian was standing there, in the same spot he'd been when she first arrived, gazing out the window, his hands clasped behind his back.

"I CAN'T BELIEVE you left it like that." Cathy was outraged, pacing Jessica's living room like a caged tiger. She hadn't been able to stand still from the moment Jessica had told her about her last meeting with Damian.

"What did you expect me to say to him?" Jessica demanded in irritation. The romantic part of her had been hoping Damian would come after her, but he hadn't. Even Evan had seemed resigned to her wishes. She'd spent one of the most emotionally draining days of her life, and the last thing she needed was chastisement from her best friend. "If he had a shred of feeling for me, this would have been a golden opportunity for him to say something, don't you think?"

"You don't want to know what I think about that man," Cathy muttered darkly.

"The best he was willing to do was a letter of recommendation. I don't need to be hit over the head, Cathy. Damian Dryden simply doesn't care about me." Kneeling before the coffee table, she jerked a piece of pizza from the box with such force the cheese slid off the top.

"Does he know you're not seeing Evan?"

"Of course he knows."

"How can you be so sure? Did you tell him?"

"No."

Cathy lifted her hands in abject frustration. "Then that's it. He thinks you're still dating his brother."

"Evan's gone out with Nadine Powell twice this week. Damian knows that. Besides, all Evan and I have ever been is friends. I told Damian that. Obviously he's not interested one way or the other, so there's no point in discussing it, is there?"

Cathy dropped onto the carpet and reached for a slice of pizza. "I'm really disappointed."

"So am I." That was a gross understatement, but Jessica had never been one to dwell on past mistakes. It would be a long time before she could consider loving Damian a mistake. She'd learned several lessons about herself, and love, in the process. When all was said and done she was going to miss him dreadfully.

"I thought you told me you and Evan were going sailing this weekend?" Cathy asked curiously.

"Not this weekend. Next."

"Aha!" Her friend slapped the end of the coffee table with her free hand. "So you *are* continuing to see Evan. Damian must know that, too. No wonder he's—"

"Cathy," Jessica said, cutting her off, "leave it. I probably won't be seeing Damian again, and apparently that's the way he wants it. Heaven knows I couldn't have been any more obvious about how I felt."

Cathy shook her head sadly. "I guess I must be more of a romantic than I realized. I was so sure he was in love with you. I was so confident I was right, I guess, because I wanted to be. I've waited all these years for you to fall in love, and now that you have..." Her voice faded as a frown ruled her features. "I was so very sure," she whispered, the puzzled expression growing more intense as though she didn't understand, even now, what could possibly have gone wrong.

"THIS IS A TREAT," Jessica said, sitting across the table from her mother in their favorite seafood restaurant. They were given a table that looked out over Back Bay. The waters were green and peaceful, and fishing boats could be seen in the distance, bobbing up and down like corks.

Joyce Kellerman spread the linen napkin on her lap and smiled serenely.

Jessica groaned inwardly. She knew that look well. It was the one that spoke of pained disappointment. Her mother had given her that identical look when she'd learned Jessica had dropped out of piano lessons. The look was there again when Jessica had refused to go to Girl Scout camp when she was twelve; it hadn't helped that her mother had been the group leader. It was her mother's way of saying Jessica's behavior completely baffled her. Jessica didn't pretend not to know what this luncheon engagement was about.

"You think I made a mistake quitting my job, don't you, Mother?"

Joyce looked mildly surprised that Jessica had introduced the subject. "I just don't understand why, that's all. It was the perfect job for you, with old family friends. You and Evan seemed to be getting along so well, and then for no reason I can discern, you resigned."

"It was time for me to move on," Jessica said vaguely.

"But you'd barely worked there two months," Joyce protested. "It doesn't look good on a résumé for you to be hopping from one job to the next. You know what your father has to say about such behavior."

There it was, in black and white, with the emphasis on black. She'd disappointed her father, the man who'd devoted his life to the preservation of her happiness.

"Working for the Drydens had become ... uncomfortable, Mom." Jessica didn't explain further. What could she say?

Her mother reached for the menu and focused her attention there. "Lois and I blame ourselves for this, you know. We were both so excited when you and Evan hit it off that we let our imaginations run away with us. Here we were talking about a wedding and grandchildren, and you two had barely started dating."

"Mom, it wasn't that."

Joyce set the menu aside and clutched the edge of the table, leaning toward Jessica. "I feel so badly about all this. I do hope you'll accept my apology, Jessica."

"Mom, listen to me. Evan and I were never romantically interested in each other. He's in love with someone else. We've had several long talks, and he's simply not ready to become involved in another relationship. That's perfectly understandable."

"Oh, dear, I'm sorry I'm late." A flustered Lois Dryden approached their table, surprising Jessica. This was her first week away from the Dryden law firm, and when her mother had suggested lunch, it had sounded like a great way to kill a couple of hours between job interviews, the very ones Damian had arranged for her. Jessica hadn't realized Damian's mother had been invited to this luncheon, as well.

"With the primary less than three weeks away, I don't think I've ever been busier." Lois Dryden pulled out a chair and sat down next to her friend and neighbor.

"Mom didn't mention you'd be joining us," Jessica said, casting a mild accusatory glance at her mother. The last thing she needed now was another inquisition.

"I hope you don't mind," Lois murmured contritely. "It does look as though we're ganging up on you, doesn't it? We don't mean to, dear. It's just that we can't help being curious about what's going on between you and Evan."

So, her mother wasn't the only one looking for answers. Lois Dryden, too. And the pair *were* ganging up on her.

"We're both far snoopier than we should be," Lois Dryden went on breathlessly, setting her small handbag next to her silverware, "but that's just part of being a mother."

"Jessica was telling me that Evan's still in love with someone else," Joyce explained.

"Oh, dear," Lois said wistfully, "I was afraid of that. Is it that Summerhill girl he was so keen on a few months ago?"

Jessica looked out over the sun-brightened waters of Back Bay and sighed. "Please understand, I don't mean to be rude, but Evan and I are friends, and I don't feel comfortable sharing what he said to me in confidence."

Joyce Kellerman beamed proudly at her friend. "My goodness, she sounds just like an attorney, doesn't she?"

"That's what she gets from hanging around my sons too long," Damian's mother replied. She crossed her

arms and leaned on the table, her expression regretful. "I'm afraid I made a terrible mistake when Evan
brought Mary Jo out to the house to meet Walter and
me."

"I can't imagine your doing anything to offend
anyone," Joyce said loyally.

"She was a shy little thing, and it was easy to see
that Walter and I made her decidedly uncomfortable.
After dinner, I tried to put her at ease, and I'm afraid
I made a miserable job of it. You see, it's vital that
Evan marry the . . . right kind of woman."

"Right kind of woman?" Jessica echoed, a little
confused. She'd known the Drydens most of her life.
They weren't snobs. They were two of the most generous conscientious people she'd ever met.

"Sometime in the future, Evan is destined to enter
the political arena," Lois explained. "Being a politi-
cian's wife is like being married to a minister. I should
know. After the last few weeks, I've been left with the
feeling that *I* am the one running for the Senate, not
Walter."

Jessica looked puzzled. "To the best of my knowledge Evan's never said anything about being interested in politics."

"Perhaps not recently, but he was keen on it before, and we've talked about it a lot in the past. It's
only been in the past year or so that his interest has
waned."

"You said all this to Mary Jo?" Joyce asked.

Lois nodded, her eyes betraying her remorse. "I've
thought back on our conversation a hundred times,
and I see now that I did more harm than good."

"Does Evan know what you said to her?" Jessica questioned.

"I'm fairly certain she didn't repeat it. I've thought of contacting her since then, thinking if I apologized she might find it in her heart to forgive me for being so terribly presumptuous."

Jessica groaned inwardly. This new information explained much of what had happened between Mary Jo and Evan, but it was too late. Mary Jo was married now, wasn't she? To that other teacher?

"I feel like I'm responsible for ruining things between you and Evan, as well," Lois went on. "I do try to stay out of my sons' lives, honestly I do, but I don't seem to have much success. I do hope you'll forgive Walter and me for pressuring you and Evan."

"Mrs. Dryden, please, you aren't at fault."

"You're such a dear girl, and Walter and I hoped it would work out between you and Evan." She paused to reach for the menu. "You make a handsome couple."

"Thank you."

The waiter came and took their order, and Lois fully relaxed. "Something's bothering Damian," she remarked. "I've tried to ask him about it, but you know Damian. He's as closemouthed as his father. Evan, bless his heart, is more like me. I've always known what Evan's thinking—well, until recently—because he's so open about his feelings. Not so with Damian."

"What about Damian?" Jessica asked, making the question sound as casual as she could.

"You could probably explain more to me than I can to you, dear," Lois said. "You see him far more often than I do, or at least, you did."

"I . . . Damian didn't make a practice of confiding in me."

Lois sighed noisily. "I figured as much. Mark my words, there's a woman involved in this. Damian may be as tight-lipped as his father, but I know my son. I think he might have fallen in love."

Jessica glanced back at the water, knowing that if Damian's mother was right, the woman was someone else. Not her.

"ONCE ON BOARD, you can go below and unload the groceries," Evan instructed, as they walked along the floating dock at the marina. When they reached the berth where the thirty-foot sailboat was moored, Evan helped Jessica aboard.

While she went below, Evan moved forward and busied himself with the sails, setting the jib and readying the spinnaker.

"It looks to me like you packed enough food for a week," Jessica shouted through the open stairwell that led to the deck above. The day was lovely, the wind perfect for sailing. Despite all his comments about being the captain while she was the crew, Evan seemed eager to do the majority of the work. Putting away a few bags of groceries seemed a paltry task.

"I'll probably set sail while you're below," Evan shouted down to her, "so don't be concerned if you feel the boat move."

Jessica's experience as a sailor was limited. Evan had insisted for weeks that he was going to change all that. Before the end of the day, he claimed she'd be a top-notch mariner. Apparently the lessons started in the galley.

Humming as she worked, Jessica unloaded the three large grocery bags. They were apparently going to eat well this weekend. She was busy cleaning radishes when she heard voices up above, but although she craned her neck to see who Evan was speaking to, she couldn't see anyone. It was probably someone standing on the dock, Jessica decided.

A few moments later came the sound of the sailboat's small outboard motor. The boat dipped slightly as Evan moved ahead and raised the sails. When the motor stopped, she knew they were a safe distance from the marina.

She finished her tasks and, bringing a couple of cans of cold soda with her, climbed up from the galley. It wasn't until she looked away from the helm that she realized someone else had joined them.

Damian.

She cast an accusatory look in Evan's direction, but it was nothing compared to the look Damian sent his way.

"I didn't know Evan had invited you," she said.

"I didn't know he'd invited *you*," Damian returned, his voice cut by the wind. The boat tilted to one side and sliced through the water.

"Evan?" Jessica glared at the man she'd once considered a friend.

Evan was grinning broadly, clearly pleased with his own cleverness. "Didn't I mention Damian would be coming along?" he asked innocently.

"No," she answered, handing each brother a can of soda and retreating to the galley. Evan was pretending the situation was the result of miscommunication, but she knew he'd purposely set it up.

Damian followed her below a few minutes later. She was sitting at the booth, her back against the side of the boat and her legs stretched out on the upholstered seat. Her arms were crossed over her chest as she tried to take in what was happening.

Damian didn't look any happier with this turn of events than she did. Walking over to the refrigerator, he replaced the can of soda she'd given him as though that had been his sole purpose in coming below.

"I think you should know I didn't arrange this meeting, if that's what you're thinking."

Jessica had nothing to say. She wasn't angry with Damian; he'd been just as manipulated as she had. She didn't know what game Evan was playing, but she wanted no part of it.

"I imagine having me around ruins your day with my brother," Damian said in what sounded strangely like an apology. He investigated the cupboards as if searching for something to eat. He brought out a bag of potato chips. "Have you found another job yet?"

"Not yet, but I've been called in for a second interview." She doubted this was news to Damian. From what she'd gathered at the new firm, he'd made her sound like God's gift to the legal profession, which was going to be one hell of a reputation to maintain.

"Do you mind if I ask you something?" she said.

"Of course not." He slipped into the narrow booth across from her.

"If you thought so highly of me, why'd you accept my resignation?" Not an entirely fair question, she realized, since she'd been the one to quit.

"Did you want me to ask you to stay?"

She smiled and shrugged. "I guess in a way I did, although it's difficult to admit that now."

"Why did you decide to quit?" He opened the bag of potato chips and offered it to her. Jessica took a handful of chips and dumped them on the tabletop, grateful for something to occupy her hands.

"Why did I decide to quit?" she said, repeating his question thoughtfully. He wasn't going to like her answer. "Mainly because of what happened at that dinner party."

Damian's dark eyes glittered with indignation. "Then it did have something to do with the attention Evan paid Nadine."

"No," she flared back. "I quit because of the pressure I felt from both sets of parents. They practically had me and Evan engaged."

"You could do far worse than marrying my brother."

"How can you even suggest such a thing?" she demanded, her voice quavering. She'd never marry a man she didn't love. "What's the matter with you, Damian?"

"With me?"

"Did you or did you not hear me in the kitchen of your parents' home less than three weeks ago?"

He frowned. "Yes." The word was clipped and angry.

"Then how can you ask me something so stupid?"

Damian's eyes were furious. He wasn't the kind of man to take kindly to insults.

Jessica grabbed a potato chip and shoved it into her mouth. Crunching down on something crisp and salty seemed to help vent her frustration.

"But Evan—"

"If you so much as suggest that Evan's in love with me," she interrupted, "I swear I won't be responsible for what I say or do next."

Damian looked taken aback by her angry retort. He closed his mouth and frowned heavily. Reaching for the potato chips, he munched on two or three, and for a moment this was the only sound in the galley.

"You know my problem, don't you?" she said.

"You mean you only have one?" Damian asked with honey-coated sarcasm.

Jessica ignored the comment. "It's that I assumed a man who had passed the bar and was one of the most brilliant minds in corporate law in Boston today, would—"

"How's everything going down there?" Evan called down. "Are you two talking yet?"

Jessica looked up to find that the younger Dryden brother had opened the door to the galley and was sitting almost directly above them, his arm on the helm, steering the sailboat. The wind ruffled his hair and flattened his windbreaker to his chest.

"We're trading insults!" Damian called back.

"That's a good place to start." Evan sounded disgustingly cheerful. "There's something you should know," he added. "I don't have any intention of turning this boat around until you two have reached an agreement."

"About what?" Jessica demanded.

"We'll get to that in a moment. Now, Damian, admit you're in love with Jessica and be done with it. Quit playing these ridiculous games."

"Damian in love with me?" she repeated incredulously. "Not a chance."

"So that's the way it's going to be," Evan called down. "Not to worry, I packed enough food to last us a good three or four days."

"Don't be absurd." Damian was beginning to sound impatient.

"Listen up, big brother," Evan shouted. "You didn't think I saw you the day you kissed Jessica in Mom's kitchen, but I did. You're crazy about her. What I can't figure out is why you insist on hiding it."

"You were the one dating her."

"So?"

"I don't get involved with women you're dating."

"There's always an exception to the rule. Jessica's a free woman. If you're in love with her, like I suspect, then why didn't you say something?"

Damian's mouth thinned. "You wouldn't understand."

"Try me," Evan insisted.

"Listen, you two," Jessica said, interrupting the exchange. "If you don't mind, I'd rather you didn't discuss me like I wasn't here."

Both men ignored her.

"Jessica's been crazy about you since she was a kid," Damian declared.

"So?" Evan returned. "She grew up and fell in love with you. A woman can change her mind if she wants. They've been known to do that."

"But you love her!" Damian insisted impatiently.

"You're right—like a sister. She'd make a terrific sister-in-law. We get along great."

Damian's eyes, which were now fixed on Jessica, grew dark and intense. "Were you about to tell me you love me?" he asked her in a husky murmur.

"Yes, you imbecile! What do I have to do—hit you over the head?"

"I don't mean to be offering you advice, big brother," Evan shouted down, "but this might be a good time to kiss her."

"I appreciate the help, *little* brother, but I can take it from here," Damian hollered back and slipped out of the booth. He shut the galley door and bolted it, then turned to Jessica.

He was grinning, she noticed, as if he'd just found out he was holding the winning ticket in the state lottery. "You must have thought I was a stubborn fool," he said, grasping her ankles and tugging her across the length of the upholstered bench. Then he gripped her around the waist and brought her upright and into his arms.

"Do you love me, Damian?" she asked.

"Heart and soul," he admitted as his hands framed her face.

"You might have said something sooner, you know," she murmured, thinking there'd been ample opportunity.

"I didn't dare. I assumed Evan loved you and needed you, but I was wrong, Jessica, very wrong. In the past few weeks I've discovered how very much I loved and needed you myself." He stroked her hair as though he couldn't believe even now that she was with him.

His mouth found hers. She wrapped her arms around him and leaned her weight into his. Damian kissed her again and again, until she was breathless with wonder. Until she marveled at how she'd managed to survive this long outside of his arms.

"I can't believe I'm holding you like this," he whispered between kisses. He couldn't seem to get enough of her, which was fine with Jessica, because she couldn't get enough of him, either.

"You're a fool, Damian Dryden."

"I know, but not any longer. I thought I was doing the noble thing by stepping aside for Evan. I was furious with him after the dinner party, but even more furious with myself."

"Why?"

"For being unable to resist holding you." His grip around her tightened. She felt the even rise and fall of his chest and nestled closer.

"You let me walk out of your life," she said, remembering the pain of leaving the law firm.

"I let you walk out of my office," he said, pressing his jaw against her hair, "but not out of my life. Never that. I was waiting, rather impatiently, to see what developed between you and my brother."

A loud knock from above finally separated them. Continuing to hold her, Damian raised one arm to unhook the latch and raise the door. "Yes?" he asked impatiently.

"Can I turn this boat around yet?"

"Not yet!" Jessica shouted.

"Give us a few more minutes," Damian added.

Evan chuckled. "Just promise me one thing," he insisted. "No, make that two."

"All right," Damian said, apparently in a generous mood.

"First, I insist on being best man at the wedding."

"Wedding," Jessica repeated slowly.

Damian nodded insistently. "The sooner the better. I've been waiting for you far too long already."

"Am I going to be best man or not?" Evan demanded.

"There's no one else I'd even consider, little brother."

"And second," Evan said with a hearty sigh, "I want to be there when you tell Mom and Dad Jessica's marrying you, instead of me."

CHAPTER TEN

"I'D FEEL BETTER if you kissed me first," Jessica murmured, looking up at Damian. They'd called the Drydens from the marina and asked Lois to invite the Kellermans over, as well.

"If you don't kiss her, I will," Evan teased, eyeing his older sibling.

"Not this time, little brother." Damian wrapped his arm around Jessica's shoulders and gently kissed her. It would have been easy to continue had they been elsewhere. Being held and kissed by Damian was the closest Jessica had ever come to paradise, and it was difficult to break away from the tender shelter of his arms.

"I don't know why I'm so nervous," Jessica said as they headed, hand in hand, toward the parking lot.

"I do." Of late, Evan seemed to be the one with all the answers. "Both sets of parents think you're marrying me." He laughed cheerfully. Clearly he was looking forward to this meeting.

Evan had been the one who insisted they talk to all four parents immediately. Damian and Jessica had agreed, but now Jessica wished she'd suggested they return to her apartment first. She needed to change clothes. Her hair was wind-tossed, and her face was red from the sun and wind.

But Damian seemed eager for this meeting, as if he, too, wanted the matter cleared with both sets of parents. He raised Jessica's hand to his mouth and brushed his lips over her knuckles.

"Don't look so worried. Mom and Dad are going to be ecstatic."

She wasn't concerned about his parents' reaction, or hers for that matter. Neither set would object to her marrying Damian. They'd be thrilled. It was just that the idea of Damian's loving her was still so new she was afraid it wasn't real.

Jessica rode with Damian, and Evan followed in his car. They got separated on the freeway, and when they pulled into the long winding drive that led to Whispering Willows, Jessica noticed Evan's car was already parked out front.

"The speed demon," Damian commented with a chuckle. He parked behind his brother, turned off the ignition and reached for Jessica, kissing her soundly. "Are you ready to walk into the dragons' den?"

She smiled and nodded, thinking she'd follow Damian anywhere.

He helped her out of the car, tucking her hand in the bend in his arm, and they walked together into the family home. The elder Drydens and Kellermans stared back at them with a look of anxious interest.

"Hello, everyone," Damian said, leading Jessica to a chair in the massive living room. He seated her and then stood directly behind her, his hands resting on her shoulders. She raised her fingers and placed them over his.

"I imagine you're wondering why we asked you here," Jessica said to her parents. Her mother sat studying Jessica as if trying to figure out what was wrong with this picture.

"Hold on!" Evan shouted from the kitchen. "Don't say another word until I get there."

"Son?" Walter Dryden gave Damian a puzzled look. "What's the meaning of this?"

"Okay, now," Evan instructed breathlessly, carrying in a silver tray with seven crystal flutes and two bottles of champagne.

"I've asked you to be here, Mr. and Mrs. Kellerman," Damian began formally, "to request the honor of marrying your daughter."

Hamilton Kellerman's face wrinkled with confusion as he turned to his wife. "You told me she was marrying Evan."

"She's—I mean, we hoped—" Joyce stammered.

"I'm in love with Damian," Jessica broke in.

Her father scratched his head. "That's not the way I remember it. You were crazy over Evan for years. Last I heard, you were making a damned nuisance of yourself."

"Daddy, that was years ago."

"She's crazy about *me* now," Damian interjected, lightly squeezing her shoulders. "And I feel the same way about her."

"Oh, Damian." Lois Dryden covered her mouth with her fingers. "We're delighted. Just delighted. Joyce, think of it, we'll be sharing grandchildren, after all."

The two women were hugging each other and dancing around in circles as Evan passed out champagne glasses to the silent confused fathers.

"You know what this is all about, Walter?"

"Can't say that I do, Ham."

"You object?"

"Hell, no. I haven't seen that much life in Lois in fifteen years. What about you? Would you rather Jessica married someone else?"

"Heavens, no." Hamilton shook his head as if he didn't know what to think. "The wife's been talking about a union between our two families all summer, only she thought it would be between Jessica and Evan. The way I figure it, a union is a union, and the two of them certainly look to be in love."

"Yes, they undoubtedly have the look," Walter said, smiling at them.

The sound of an exploding cork echoed about the room as Evan uncorked a bottle of champagne. "I'd like to propose a toast," he said, walking from person to person filling the flutes. "To Jessica and Damian," he said, setting the bottle aside and holding up his glass. "May their lives always be filled with happy surprises, and may their love endure for all time."

"Evan, how sweet," Lois said, dabbing the corner of her eye.

"For all time," Joyce agreed.

Everyone raised their glasses, then took a sip of champagne.

"Now, let's talk about the wedding," Lois said, prepared then and there to square away the details. She sat on the sofa next to her husband.

"It'll have to be after the November election," Joyce commented thoughtfully.

"We need to make it through the September primary first," Lois said. "I can't see delaying the wedding when we don't know for certain Walter will be in contention for the Senate."

"Nonsense. Of course he'll be on the ballot."

"Does any of this matter to you?" Damian asked Jessica, leaning so that his lips were close to her ear. A warm tingling sensation raced down her arms.

She smiled softly and shook her head. Nothing mattered except Damian and his love. "I'd marry you tomorrow if we could arrange it."

Damian drew in a deep breath. "Don't tempt me, sweetheart."

"Or in six months, if that's necessary. I've waited for you all my life, Damian. A few more weeks isn't going to matter."

Their mothers would have it all arranged within the hour, Jessica guessed. Their fathers were talking, too, working out schedules and other necessary details. The two families had been friends through all the seasons of their lives. The same way their own love—hers and Damian's—would last, weathering all the ups and downs the years would bring.

Jessica felt as though she'd come to the end of a long journey. She was home now, secure in Damian's love.

EPILOGUE

As Evan Dryden set aside the brief he was preparing and pinched the bridge of his nose, there was a knock on his door. Glad of the interruption, he called, "Come in."

His brother entered. The changes in Damian in the months since he'd married Jessica were many. Evan remembered a time when practicing law ruled Damian's life. He worked after hours and weekends, rarely taking time away. But now his brother looked younger, happier and so damn much in love Evan couldn't help a twinge of jealousy.

Witnessing the changes in Damian caused him to wonder what his own life would have been like if he'd married Mary Jo. They'd have started a family by now. The glimpse he'd caught of her almost a year ago at the Red Sox game drifted into his mind, and with it came a stab of pain.

Loving her as he did, even now, it was impossible to want anything but the best for her. He tried not to think about Mary Jo, tried to place her firmly in the back of his mind, but every now and again, the memory of her escaped to taunt him with the might-have-beens.

It had been nearly eighteen months since they'd parted, and she still had the power to move him. He'd dated now and again, but there wasn't anyone he'd gotten serious about. He wished he knew what it was about Mary Jo that he couldn't forget.

Evan envied his brother the happiness he'd found and didn't expect to find the same happiness himself. He could see himself thirty years down the road with white hair, dressed in a smoking jacket, sitting in front of a fireplace smoking a pipe. A black Labrador would lie snoozing at his feet....

"You're looking thoughtful," Damian said, helping himself to a chair.

"Just wool-gathering."

Damian was more relaxed these days, Evan noted. His brother leaned back in the chair and rested one ankle over the other knee. "Remember last month when Jessica phoned from the doctor's office?"

Evan chuckled. "I'm not likely to forget." Nor would anyone else in the office. Rarely had he seen his brother so excited, so elated. For days he'd walked around grinning like a mad fool. It wasn't every day, he said, a man learned he was going to be a father.

Funny, Evan thought, his brother was wearing a similar grin now. "What's going on now?" he asked. "Did you just learn Jessica's carrying twins?"

"Not quite. I've been approached by the bar about an appointment as a judge."

"Damian!" Evan rose from his chair. This shouldn't come as a surprise; it was Damian's destiny, just as marrying Jessica had been. He walked around his desk. Damian stood and the two brothers embraced.

"You're going to accept." Evan didn't put the words into a question. It went without saying Damian would and should.

"Yes, if Jessica concurs."

"She will." Evan had no doubts about that, either. "Are you going out tonight to celebrate?"

"As a matter of fact we are. Cathy Hudson, Jessica's friend, is starring in a new play that's opening tonight. Did I mention she recently got engaged to some director friend of hers?"

Before Evan could respond, his intercom buzzed and he reached for the button. "The receptionist called," Mrs. Sterling informed him, "and said Earl Kress is here to see you, Mr. Dryden."

"Earl?" Evan said with surprise. He hadn't heard from him in six months or more. "Send him in."

"We'll talk later," Damian said as he walked out of the office. "Give my regards to Earl, will you?"

Evan went with him, meeting Earl in the hallway outside. The two exchanged hearty handshakes. Evan slapped the younger man on the back as he led him into his office and closed the door.

"It's good to see you," Evan said, motioning toward the chair. "Sit down and make yourself comfortable."

"I can't stay long," Earl said, sitting on the edge of the chair. "I probably should have called, but I was in the neighborhood . . ."

"I'm glad you stopped in. How's school?"

"Good. I got my general equivalency diploma not long ago," he announced proudly.

"Congratulations." Evan experienced a surge of pride at the younger man's progress.

"I have a lot of people to thank for that, but you're the one who started it all. I don't think you ever realized how afraid I was of having the world know I couldn't read or write. It's humiliating to admit something like that."

"I realized at the time how difficult it was for you."

"Without your support, I don't think I could have gone through with the trial."

"I'm sure glad you did."

"Yeah, me, too," Earl said with a hearty laugh. "My life would certainly be different if I hadn't. Listen, I didn't mean to take up your time, but I wanted you to know how grateful I am for all your help."

"No problem, Earl."

"I'm working as a volunteer myself now with grade-school kids, helping out in the slow-reader program. I wouldn't have grown up illiterate if I'd gotten help while I was in the elementary grades."

Evan smiled broadly. "That's great, Earl."

"By the way, I ran across a friend of yours the other day—another volunteer."

"Oh?"

"At least I assume you two know one another. Her name's Mary Jo Summerhill."

"Mary Jo." Evan realized he breathed her name more than spoke it.

"Funny, she reacted the same way when I mentioned you."

"I thought she was married," Evan said.

"Not as far as I know." Earl stood and held out his hand. "Anyway, I won't keep you. I just wanted to stop in and update you about what's been going on in my life."

"I'm happy you did," Evan said, walking his former client to the door. He stood there for a moment, his mind spinning.

A few minutes later Damian strolled into his office again.

"What did Earl have to say?" he asked.

"Mary Jo isn't married." He said it out loud just to hear the sound of it. Damian wouldn't fully understand the significance of those words, but it didn't matter.

"I see," his brother said thoughtfully. "What are you going to do about it?"

Evan thought long and hard, then a slow smile spread across his features.

*   *   *   *   *

Will Evan find happiness with Mary Jo?
Watch for Debbie's next Romance,
Ready for Marriage, coming in 1994, to find out!

Let

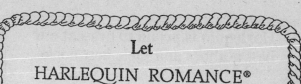

HARLEQUIN ROMANCE®

take you

BACK TO THE

Come to SkyRim Ranch in Bison County, Nebraska!

Meet Abbie Hale, rancher's daughter—a woman who loves her family ranch and loves the ranching life. *Then meet Yates Connley*, the stranger who comes to SkyRim for Christmas....

Read Bethany Campbell's
The Man Who Came for Christmas,
our next Back to the Ranch title.
Available in December
wherever Harlequin books are sold.

RANCH7

Harlequin is proud to present our best authors and their best books. Always the best for your reading pleasure!

Throughout 1993, Harlequin will bring you exciting books by some of the top names in contemporary romance!

In November, look for

BARBARA DELINSKY

First, Best and Only

Their passion burned even stronger....

CEO Marni Lange didn't have time for nonsense like photographs. The promotion department, however, insisted she was the perfect cover model for the launch of their new career-woman magazine. She couldn't argue with her own department. She should have.

The photographer was a man she'd prayed never to see again. Brian Webster had been her first— and best—lover. This time, could she play with fire without being burned?

Don't miss FIRST, BEST AND ONLY by Barbara Delinsky... wherever Harlequin books are sold.

Make Christmas a truly
Romantic experience—with

HARLEQUIN ROMANCE®

Wouldn't *you* love to kiss a tall, dark
Texan under the mistletoe? Gwen does,
in HOME FOR CHRISTMAS by
Ellen James. Share the experience!

Wouldn't *you* love to kiss a sexy
New Englander on a snowy Christmas
morning? Angela does, in Shannon
Waverly's CHRISTMAS ANGEL.
Share the experience!

Look for both of these Christmas
Romance titles, available in December
wherever Harlequin Books are sold.

(And don't forget that Romance novels
make great gifts! Easy to buy, easy to
wrap and just the right size for a
stocking stuffer. *And* they make a
wonderful treat when you need a break
from Christmas shopping, Christmas
wrapping and stuffing stockings!)

1993 Keepsake

CHRISTMAS
Stories

Capture the spirit and romance of Christmas with KEEPSAKE CHRISTMAS STORIES, a collection of three stories by favorite historical authors. The perfect Christmas gift!

Don't miss these heartwarming stories, available in November wherever Harlequin books are sold:

ONCE UPON A CHRISTMAS by Curtiss Ann Matlock
A FAIRYTALE SEASON by Marianne Willman
TIDINGS OF JOY by Victoria Pade

ADD A TOUCH OF ROMANCE TO YOUR HOLIDAY SEASON WITH KEEPSAKE CHRISTMAS STORIES!

HX93

**Fifty red-blooded, white-hot, true-blue hunks
from every State in the Union!**

Look for MEN MADE IN AMERICA! Written by some
of our most poplar authors, these stories feature fifty of
the strongest, sexiest men, each from a different state in
the union!

Two titles available every other month at your favorite
retail outlet.

In November, look for:

STRAIGHT FROM THE HEART by Barbara Delinsky
(Connecticut)
AUTHOR'S CHOICE by Elizabeth August (Delaware)

In January, look for:

DREAM COME TRUE by Ann Major (Florida)
WAY OF THE WILLOW by Linda Shaw (Georgia)

You won't be able to resist MEN MADE IN AMERICA!

When the only time you have for yourself is…

STOLEN moments ™

Christmas is such a busy time—with shopping, decorating, writing cards, trimming trees, wrapping gifts.…

When you do have a few *stolen moments* to call your own, treat yourself to a brand-new *short* novel. Relax with one of our Stocking Stuffers— or with all six!

Each STOLEN MOMENTS title
is a complete and original contemporary romance that's the perfect length for the busy woman of the nineties! Especially at Christmas…

And they make perfect **stocking stuffers**, too! (For your mother, grandmother, daughters, friends, co-workers, neighbors, aunts, cousins—all the other women in your life!)

Look for the STOLEN MOMENTS display in December

STOCKING STUFFERS:

HIS MISTRESS Carrie Alexander
DANIEL'S DECEPTION Marie DeWitt
SNOW ANGEL Isolde Evans
THE FAMILY MAN Danielle Kelly
THE LONE WOLF Ellen Rogers
MONTANA CHRISTMAS Lynn Russell

HSM2

WORLDWIDE LIBRARY ®